THE
SUPERIOR
GUARDIAN

THE
SUPERIOR
GUARDIAN

George Griesinger

Published by
Illumify Media Global
www.IllumifyMedia.com
"Let's bring your book to life!"

Library of Congress Control Number: applied for

Paperback ISBN: 978-1-964251-90-5
Hardcover ISBN: 978-1-964251-91-2

Typeset by Art Innovations (http://www.artinnovations.in/)
Cover design by Susan Nachtrieb and Debbie Lewis

Printed in the United States of America

To my father, the patriarch of our family, who,
like Abraham of old, left behind his kindred and
homeland, bravely leading us on a perilous journey
across thousands of miles to an unknown land
of promise. His courage carved a path through
uncertainty, and his faith laid the foundation
beneath my feet.

Now I walk that path, not only as a son, but as a
guardian of the legacy he began—to protect what is
sacred, to speak what is true, and to carry the light
forward for those yet to come.

CONTENTS

PROLOGUE

Lake Superior, one of the largest and most pristine freshwater lakes in the world, offers visitors everything from nature's raw power to the peaceful calm of a walk along a beach. Yet few of today's visitors know of a historic battle that once threatened this great lake's future.

Near Silver Bay, Minnesota, the Reserve Mining Company discharged tons of fine sediment into the lake daily over a span of twenty-five years. The water near the plant became persistently murky, gray green.

When the newly formed U.S. Environmental Protection Agency (EPA) investigated the impact of Reserve's operations on the lake in the early 1970s, an alarming discovery was made: cancer-causing fibers had made their way into Duluth's drinking water sixty miles away.

In a landmark ruling, a court ordered the Reserve to stop the dumping, setting a national precedent that the government could require industry to clean up its act.

But this story begins even earlier. Two years before the EPA existed, in the shadow of Silver Bay's rising conflict, a seventeen-year-old local boy named George faced a trial of his own. His only crime? Standing up for a conviction. His ambition? To protect the lake that had shaped his soul and strengthened his character.

Lake Superior was more than water and waves to him. It was a place of refuge, a keeper of secrets, and the only thing that understood the sorrow he carried. It became his confidant, his comforter, and his cause. But the price of being the lake's champion would be high. This is the story of that boy—and the price he paid.

1

HUMBLE BEGINNING

The echoes of war still whispered through the cobblestone streets, mingling with the laughter of young boys at play. It was the 1950s, a time when the country was still recovering from a shattered past. Yet in a quaint village nestled in a river valley cradled by rolling hills and lush meadows time had paused. Though the conflict had devastated Germany and the city of Stuttgart just thirty miles to the north, no visible scars remained here.

Hidden among the craggy hills were the ruins of a castle fortress, frozen in time from another era. The innocence of childhood colored every moment, filling the hearts of those who lived here with quiet joy.

Life flowed at a gentle pace, untouched by the horrors of the outside world, resembling a medieval romance painted in vibrant tones. The castle ruins, the winding orchards, and the meadows framed a horizon both dreamlike and familiar. Imagine knights galloping down dirt paths, their laughter mixing with the rustling leaves. Here, the past was a muse, and the present wrote its stories in the laughter, love, and simplicity of cherished memories.

The way of life for peasant farmers from centuries past still shapes life. Though the streets were paved, most remained cobblestone or dirt. Cars—used mostly by visitors passing through—were as rare here as horse-drawn carriages are in modern cities. There was little need for them. Everything in Dettingen was within reach by foot, bicycle, or wagon.

The village sat at the lowest point of a rich valley—a *Tal*—surrounded by fields, orchards, forests, and the rocky *Schwäbische Alb*. Every path out was uphill. Villagers lived in tightly clustered homes and worked their *Wiese*, or fields, scattered across the surrounding land.

During harvest season, it was easy to forget what century you were in. Farmers picked apples and loaded them into horse-drawn wagons stacked six to eight feet high, just as they had for generations. For Wolfgang and me, this season was pure magic. We climbed into Ähni's cherry trees—*Ähni* being the Schwäbisch name we used for Opa or grandfather—picking, eating, and decorating ourselves with the vibrant red fruit. With cherries dangling from our ears, we chewed mouthfuls and spit the pits at each other in sticky games of tag that would make any modern sanitation inspector faint.

The trip to Ähni's Wiese during the harvest was an exhilarating adventure, the kind that throbbed with promise as we ascended the rolling hills in Ähni's creaky, empty horse-drawn wagon. The ride in our medieval convertible was delightful, a whimsical pause before the day's labor began. But after hours of plucking sun-drenched apples under the warm embrace of the autumn sun, the journey home morphed into a daunting challenge.

The slope, though gentle, transformed into a formidable challenge beneath the heavy bounty of apples that filled our wagon to the brim. Each bump felt like a wild descent down a cliff, sending ripples of fear through our hearts. This clearly was no place for carefree laughter, so we decided to abandon our seat and follow the wagon on foot, our senses heightened by the thrill of navigating the precarious path ahead. The apple-laden wagon rumbled ominously in front of us, and each creak echoed the exhilaration of our adventure.

The adults accompanying the harvest walked alongside the wagon with us, doing what they could to break the heavy load when needed. On occasion, an eerie premonition of what could happen occurred when the wagon wheels found a pothole. The disturbance was enough to spill apples off the wagon as a harbinger of what could happen on a larger scale. This gave everyone pause, and they had lumps in their throats, adding drama to the trip home. Later, when the tales were retold and embellished, they made for spellbinding intrigue.

Ähni, the experienced wagon master, always brought the horse, wagon, and delectable load of apples into town safely. What followed was spectacular. Ähni delivered his wagonload of fresh, succulent fruit to the community apple press. The entire load of apples was dumped into a big hopper that fed the press.

This was an annual event worthy of being posted on the calendar. All the kids looked forward to it with great anticipation. The sweet smell of apple nectar permeated the air and our senses. With unwavering patience, we waited for the fruit of our labor to flow out of the press like a spring of honey-sweet liquid refreshment. It is easy to imagine children in medieval times, standing around this press, waiting for the same refreshing elixir to flow out and rejuvenate them from a hard day's work.

The entire load of apples was pressed. Ähni had several one-hundred-gallon wooden kegs on hand. These kegs were filled with freshly squeezed apple juice. He then brought them back to his place and rolled them into his cellar. That was where the celebration continued as we drank our fill of fresh apple juice until our stomachs hurt. Nothing surpassed the taste of fresh apple juice, harvested mere hours after the apples were sun-ripening on the tree.

Everyone drank their fill, well, almost everyone. Ähni was the exception. He always held back. His temperance at the time was understandable, even for a six-year-old. He wanted to wait for the good stuff.

After several months the apple juice fermented and transformed into Ähni's favorite beverage, Most, a Schwäbisch term for hard cider. That is when his celebration started, and it kept going until the last keg ran dry. It was an adult beverage by then. The sour vinegar flavor had no appeal to six-year-olds. But Ähni liked it. And, it wasn't hard, even for me, to tell how much he did. Seldom would you see Ähni in his Stube, Schwäbisch for living room, without his pint-sized stein of *Most*.

Growing up, I hung around with Ahne—the Schwäbisch name we used for Oma, or grandmother— and Ähni's house. You might say I didn't have much choice. From the age of six weeks, it was Ahne who raised me. Every day, my young mother would drop me off at her house en route to the factory where she worked making leather gloves.

MY PARENTS' STORY

My mother, being a refugee from Bohemia, was an outsider in this Schwäbisch village. She grew up in Nejdek, a Sudeten German town in Bohemia, where her family lived comfortably until the end of World War II. After the war, the Germans were expelled by nomadic gypsy bands, their home was ransacked, and her treasured grand piano was chopped up for firewood. Her family was forced into a concentration camp. Because she spoke Czech, she was allowed to come and go from the camp, and she bravely smuggled food to her loved ones inside. Her father did not survive.

As the border between Czechoslovakia and Eastern Germany was closing, she made a daring nighttime escape across a stubble field with her stepbrother, slipping past armed guards with machine guns. Carrying with her little more than faith and resolve, she was one of the last refugees to cross into Germany before the Iron Curtain was erected. As a refugee, she responded to an ad and found work sewing leather gloves in the small village where my father grew up.

My father grew up in Dettingen, where life was sheltered even during the war. During the war, he was required to join the Hitlerjugend, as most boys were. After the war, he was apprenticed and worked as an electrician. When he wasn't working, he did what many young German men did—he spent his evenings in the local beer hall.

It was there, in that ordinary place, that his path crossed with my mother. He, a tradesman seeking simple companionship, found her music—and her courage—unforgettable. Out of that unlikely meeting of two vastly different worlds, my family's story began.

The living quarters where my father grew up were now my day care center. It had a large barn at the rear for Ähni's farm animals. The house itself was constructed directly adjacent to the street that ran in front. There was neither a front yard nor a sidewalk, as the street served as the sidewalk. In the post-war era, Dettingen was a reminder of how villages were built and looked in medieval times. Not only were there few cars, but many modern appliances were also either rare or nonexistent. High-tech electronic devices were fifty years away. Many low-tech items, such as simple black-and-white televisions, radios, or even toasters, were also difficult to find. There were few, if any, telephones, stereos, no automatic dishwashers, and even washing machines were scarce.

Clothes were hand washed by kneading them in large metal tubs filled with hot, soapy water. The rinse cycle took place in another tub of clean water, and then they were wrung out by hand and hung on the clothesline to dry. The most significant transformation in Dettingen from its medieval era to the 1950s was the arrival of electricity. This advancement enabled nighttime illumination and powered the few electrical appliances, such as basic refrigerators.

My day care center, run by Ahne, was stark. In this simple yet profound space, my experience was shaped by the absence of electronic gadgets and games; I could scarcely fathom their existence. Without the distraction of television or the allure of music, my world was stripped down to its essentials, only a handful of cherished toys. In this quiet sanctuary, my imagination flourished, just as it would have in a time when children crafted their adventures from the threads of reality and nature surrounding them.

The toys I had were of the action variety. A hand-carved wooden top was one of my favorites. The top had grooves carved into it and came with a whip, a string attached to a small stick. To activate this toy, I wound the string tightly in the grooves of the top. With one hand holding the string to the top and the other clutching the handle of the whip, I pulled on the whip with a sharp jerk, sending the top spinning into the street.

Other kids joined in, and whenever someone's top began to slow down and wobble, briskly delivered swats with the whips brought it back to life. We played with them for hours. The last top standing and spinning would win. It was the same game kids growing up in Dettingen hundreds of years before played. Compared to modern toys, I am stunned by how simple and timeless that toy top was.

Besides drinking unfermented cider, one of the staples of my diet was the bread that Ahne baked. This was such a low-tech operation it didn't even require electricity. It is another one of those activities, like kids playing in the streets with wooden tops or pressing apples into cider, that was done the same way for hundreds of years.

KNIGHTS, CASTLES, AND DRAGONS

$\mathscr{B}$readmaking started when Ahne put large quantities of flour, water, and yeast in an oversized ceramic bowl. Using a wooden spoon, she stirred the mixture by hand until it became dough. Making bread and washing clothes is where Ahne got her arm strength, which you realized if you misbehaved or arm wrestled with her.

Later, she divided the dough into smaller bowls, covered them with linen cloths, and allowed them to rise overnight.

The next morning, as the sun rose, I was recruited as her assistant baker. My first task was to help load the bowls into a wooden wagon. Then, after I fed the chickens, Ahne joined me to start the journey to the

Backhaus, the Schwäbisch word for the village hearth. I tugged the wooden wagon, its wheels creaking under the weight of the dough, along a path to the *Backhaus*, in the center of town. As we went around a curve through a patch of birch trees, the scent of yeast and cracked grain filled the morning air.

"Ach, this reminds me," she said, brushing flour from her apron, "of a *Märchen* worth telling today." (A *Märchen* is a Schwäbisch fairy tale.) She could have stopped right there, as she didn't need to say anything more. I was already smiling.

Storytelling played a significant role in the upbringing of children in Dettingen. *Geschichten*, stories, and *Märchen*, magical fairy tales, served as the cinema of the day, long before the advent of movies. These charming narratives not only provided enchanting entertainment that children eagerly anticipated, but they also instilled good values, character, and meaningful life lessons. Passed down from generation to generation, these timeless tales were part of Schwäbisch lore.

Having grown up in a village linked to medieval times, the mythical stories of castles, knights, and dragons felt like part of everyday life. The remnants of castles, dark caves, and shadowy forests surrounded me, making me think these stories could have been real. Let's see if we can find out.

I was on the way to making fresh bread. A *Märchen* was in the wind. The ruins of a castle on a hill were in front of me. I was already living in a magical fairy tale world.

"Ah," Ahne began with a sigh that was part memory, part joy. "This is just the kind of morning for a dragon story."

"You've heard of dragons, ja?" she asked, as if we were speaking of the chickens at the house.

"Well, then, listen closely, *meine Schatze*. Let me tell you about Siegfried, a brave knight who fought one."

I slowed the wagon just enough for her to catch up. That meant I was ready to listen.

"Siegfried was no ordinary knight. He was both clever and kind, but he was also brave. Brave enough to seek out a real dragon, one that had scales as hard as iron pots and eyes that shone like lanterns in the dark."

She adjusted her apron thoughtfully as if it held a secret and then continued. "When Siegfried found the dragon, he fought for a day and a night. When the beast finally fell, its blood poured across the ground like dark wine. Siegfried was no fool; he knew there was magic in the blood. So, he bathed in it."

The wagon's wheels bumped over a root, and I adjusted my grip. Ahne leaned in.

"But—" she said, her voice dropping low, "as he stood in the blood, a single leaf drifted down from a linden tree and stuck to his back, right between his shoulder blades. That one small spot was untouched. It stayed . . . ordinary. That spot would cost him."

My mouth was already watering, not just from the smell of bread on the breeze but from the tension in her voice.

"Later, another knight—jealous and cruel—found out. And when Siegfried bent to drink from a mountain spring, this knight threw a spear. Right into that tiny, unprotected spot on his back. And just like that—"

She snapped her fingers gently. "The brave knight fell, *kaput*."

We walked in silence for a few steps.

Then she added softly, "Even the strongest can fall, my dear. Not because they aren't strong. But because someone always sees where they are soft and weak."

She reached into the wagon and tucked a corner of the linen cloth back over the rising dough.

"Now, let's hurry, or the *Backhaus* will be full and the best baking stones will be taken. Our bread is meant to be golden, not jealous."

Upon arrival, we first loaded the kiln with fuel in the form of sticks and kindling. After this burned into a hot bed of coals, we took the dough that Ahne had shaped into loaves and loaded it on shelves above the coals. The door to the kiln was shut, and we waited until our bread was ready.

Each time she swung the door open to check, a warm wave of the fragrant aroma of fresh bread washed over me, filling the air with its comforting scent. This was one of the best parts of the baking process. The fragrance of freshly baked bread wafted out of the dome-shaped structure, overwhelming my senses. My mouth salivated for the best-tasting bread I would ever eat. When it came fresh out of the kiln, the bread was loaded with so much flavor and a fresh, filling taste that it was like eating a gourmet meal. And, yes, it was golden, the way Ahne liked it.

Besides the fresh bread, the other best part of the baking operation was getting paid for being Ahne's assistant. This occurred on the way home when Ahne took a detour and passed by the village's "ice cream" shop, except ice cream was too modern for this village. The ice cream in Dettingen was what was affectionately called *Schlagsahne*, which is Schwäbisch for whipped cream.

The shop owner hand-whipped rich, fresh cream into a heavy, sweet, whipped cream and loaded it into a wafer cone. Ahne handed him five *Pfennig* and then handed me the cone. Another simple delicacy, way too delicious to describe, ended up in the favorite section of my menu. There is nothing better. I savored every lick of that cone until it was gone, and we were home. Turning the corner into her backyard, I then brought the wagon, which was loaded with loaves of fresh golden bread, into the barn.

"Ja, nice," sighed Ahne as she removed her now soiled apron and wiped her powerful arms. "We made it," she said, letting out another sigh.

I worked and got lots of exercise. I learned a skill. I had fun. And I had a delicious treat. And best of all, I had Ahne, who loved me.

When I dropped the handle of the wagon, I ran over to Ahne, wrapped my arms around her legs, and gave her a big hug of appreciation. Looking up, I saw her soft smile, turning into a big grin as a tear formed in her eye.

With Ahne at my side, I could not imagine life getting any better than this. And I didn't have to because things were about to change.

3

PARADISE LOST

*I*t was in the spring after my sixth birthday when I had a dream, though calling it a dream seems too simple. It felt more like a memory that someone else handed me. One that I wasn't supposed to have yet.

That night, I slept under the comforting cover of my feather bed, which enveloped me like a big, fluffy cloud. The hearth fire had long since burned out, and I remember the silence, the kind you get in winter when even the wind seems to freeze in place. I drifted off thinking about Ahne. She had sung to me earlier that day. Her soft voice cracked like the pages of an old hymnal.

In the dream, I wasn't in the village anymore. I was standing in a *Weise,* a meadow, I didn't recognize. It was nothing like Ähni's orchard. There was tall grass waving all around me as if the earth itself was breathing. The sun was just climbing over the edge of the hills, soft and golden, and the air smelled like spring, not the muddy kind of spring we knew in the village but something cleaner. Pristine. Something almost sacred.

That's when I saw it.

It emerged from the mouth of a cave nestled within a craggy cliff near the village, slow and silent, as if it had always existed there and was only now choosing to reveal itself. A panther. Not gray, not brown but black, like shadows piled on each other. Its back shimmered with flecks of silver like stars caught in its fur. But I didn't feel afraid. I felt… known.

It stopped just a few steps in front of me, and our eyes locked. There was something ancient in that gaze, something older than stories. Then it opened its mouth . . . and breathed.

It didn't roar. Or growl. Just took a breath.

Warm air washed over me, sweet like honey and elderflowers. The grass around us swayed as if bowing. All around me birds took flight, and for a moment I thought the sun itself shone brighter.

But then I felt it, a ripple far off in the tall grass. Something moved. Slithering. A shape low to the ground. I didn't see it clearly, but I knew it was watching.

The panther turned its head slightly in that direction, then back to me. Its eyes softened, and even though it didn't open its mouth, I heard the words "You are not alone."

Then it faded. Just like that, it dissolved into the mist.

When I woke, I was cold and sweating. My fingers clutched my featherbed so tightly that I crushed some of its feathers. Morning light spilled across the floor, and the first rays of sunlight caused the room to glow like copper. To this day, I can still see those golden eyes. And sometimes I wonder if that dream was waiting for me… for something unknown. Although my early years were locked in a time warp that had changed little in hundreds of years, change is not something that can be controlled, especially for a six-year-old boy.

In my mythical, romanticized world, I had something good. But one day, when my mother came to pick me up, I felt a disturbance that signaled a change. Something was going to happen.

"Now, why do you want to leave Dettingen and go to America?" Ahne asked my mother with concern in her voice.

"Albert thinks there are better jobs there, and they need electricians," my mother replied matter-of-factly.

Wait a minute! This does not sound good! I thought. *It sounds like my parents are moving somewhere. What and where is America?*

My ears perked up as I listened to more of their conversation. It didn't take me long to realize that this did not sound good because it wasn't. After a wave of troubling thoughts, I decided that this was not for me. I had heard all I wanted to hear, so I pulled on Ahne's dress to get her attention. "Ahne, where is America?" I asked.

"It is on the other side of the ocean," Ahne replied.

Her answer didn't help and only raised more questions. However, the tone of the conversation was troubling. That was all I needed. I decided that this America, whatever or wherever it was, was not for me.

"Mama, is America far away?" I finally burst out.

That ended their conversation full stop. I must have struck a nerve as they just stared at each other in silence for what seemed like several minutes.

Ahne then turned to me with a look that cut right through me. It told me everything I wanted to know. The concern on her face and the sadness in her eyes confirmed my worst fears. At that point, I made up my mind. I would not participate.

"Ja, it's far away. Why do you ask? You look like you are upset," Mother replied.

"Are you going to go there?" I responded in frustration. Before she could even answer, I bristled with blustery anger. "If you are, I am not going with you. I am going to stay with Ahne!"

Ahne looked at me. Tears welled up in her sad eyes as she shook her head. She looked at my mother with a puzzled look, as if to say, "Are you sure you want to do this, Doris?"

My mother then took my hand and said, "We'd better go home now. We will talk about this later," and with that we headed toward the street.

"Bye, Ahne."

The journey to our house was troubling as I was alone with my thoughts: *What is this all about? My parents and family want to move to a faraway place called America. Are they serious? Nobody does something like that here. What has gotten into them? How did this happen?* I had so many questions. But there was one sure thing, I was not going with them. No way! *I will stay and live with Ahne. And that is final. I won't go!*

To say it rocked my serene little world is a big understatement. It completely disrupted my idyllic life. I was on a different track now. I would have to grow up a little faster than I would have without this disturbing development.

I had wished I had never overheard the conversation about moving. It was a significant event, a life-changer. Absolutely! Since I was determined I wasn't going to go with them, I figured I might never see my mom, my dad, or my two younger brothers, Wolfgang, who was five and Gerhard, who was one, again. *How am I supposed to deal with that?* I wondered.

After that day, my life wasn't the same. My routine did not change. Although I was still in Ahne's care during the day and did all the simple things that went with it, it was no longer as fulfilling as it once was. I was being pulled in two directions by the fear of losing something I couldn't afford to let go. There was no winning—only breaking. I was stuck in the middle, unraveling.

Although my mind was made up regarding what I would do, I had no peace. As the time approached, my parents would frequently discuss the relocation and gently inquire about my intentions, hoping to gauge how serious I was with my decision not to join them. I held my ground, but at night, my sleep was restless. My mind would imagine when the move would happen, some months in the distance. Staying and never seeing my family again was not pleasant to think about. But leaving and never seeing Ahne and Ähni again was just as bad. However, I didn't dwell on that scenario, as my mind was made up to stay.

The only hope I had was that my parents would change their minds and decide not to go. I thought that by holding out, maybe I could change their minds. As the day of the move drew closer, it became a battle of wills.

It was a battle I would lose. They were going to go with or without me. It was difficult for me to understand that. They tried and failed to change my mind and were resigned to letting me stay and grow up with my grandparents thousands of miles away. It became personal. What were they thinking?

My parents spent a lot of time planning the move. When I found out when they were moving, fear took center stage. A date was set. February 6 they would leave Dettingen on a train to the northern German port city of Bremerhaven. There, they would board a World War II battleship, the USS *General W. G. Haan,* for the eight-day trip to America. They would arrive in New York City on February 14, Valentine's Day.

Where is the love in that? I wondered.

My world was thrown upside down. I dreaded going to sleep at night. As soon as my head hit the pillow, my cinematographic mind tortured me with idyllic images of my fairy tale world. Six years isn't long enough to be living in paradise. Without notice, another channel came on. My mind was locked on cruel images of my family leaving. They were going on a trip without me. Never to return! Going to bed was not fun.

As the days passed and February drew near, anxiety, fears, and sleepless nights affected me more. They were my constant, unwelcome companions.

My family was allowed to take one four-by-four-by-four-foot wooden crate on the ship. Whatever fit into it was all they were allowed to take with them, in addition to suitcases. Unfortunately, I had to be around for the unpleasant experience of packing, which brought the reality of this home even more. They had not even left yet, and I was feeling all alone. To protect themselves and lessen the pain of parting, it seemed as though I was already being treated as if I were no longer part of the family. I became a stranger in my own home.

Whenever they talked about the move, what to pack, or discussed what life might be like in the new country, I got left out. Since my mind was made up, they saw no need for me to be included. I understood, and yet it still hurt.

The pain, the anxieties, the fears, and the questions all affected me. As the months ticked down to weeks and the weeks to days, I grew increasingly austere. I felt abandoned, alone.

The day finally came when my mother quit her job. As a result, I spent less time at Ahne's and more around my family, even though I felt less a part of it. Suddenly it was crunch time. Two days before the move, my dad quit his job. I was over at Ahne's house, trying to be brave and hold myself together, which was impossible. Even at Ahne's, I felt all alone and, frankly, afraid. This was scarier than anything I could have imagined.

What am I doing? I thought. I had stubbornly made the decision that brought me to this place. At the time, I felt brave and bold. But now I felt weak and exposed. I realized that no matter what decision I made, the outcome would inevitably lead to a significant loss. Like in the story of Siegfried, did a linden leaf fall on my back, leaving an area where I was weak and vulnerable? That was how I felt all over. It must have been a big leaf.

My *real* family was leaving me. *Time for a reality check. Should I rethink this? No. I could not bear to leave Ahne. No!*

Enshrouded in a dense fog, I lost my ability to see. There were no reference points, and hope was vanishing. I couldn't decide.

Ahne had a strong faith, one she *lived* by. It was woven into her fairy tales like the one she told me on the path to the *Backhaus*. It showed up in how she taught me the Bible—not as a book of rules, but as the owner's manual for my life. The Psalms to care for my emotions. The Proverbs to feed my mind. And I needed both now. Desperately.

There was one Proverb that surfaced gently through the noise and confusion:

"Trust in the Lord with all your heart and lean not on your own understanding." But I was drowning in fear. The emotional weight, the trauma of impending loss, blurred everything.

I don't recall how it began, but I was already in tears when my parents arrived at Ahne's house. "What's wrong, George?" my mother asked, like they couldn't guess.

No answer. Just louder crying. We were all in Ahne's *Stube*. I was on the floor, crying. My mother, father, Ahne, and Ähni all were standing around me, unsure of what to do. Ahne knelt beside me. She stroked my hair, her eyes full of concern. "What are you feeling right now?" she whispered.

I sobbed bitterly. "Ahne, I'm scared. I don't know what to do."

Ahne's voice broke as tears filled her eyes. "This is very difficult," she said.

I raised my tear-soaked face to look at her. "I want to stay with you," I said.

She gently touched my hand. "But what about your family?"

I cried out louder. "I might never see them again!"

Ahne began to sob. "I know!" she said and broke down with me.

Still sobbing, I cried, "Ahne, I just don't know what to do! I feel alone!"

Ahne turned to my mother, who was also crying. She came down beside me and hugged me tightly.

Ahne said, "Doris, he is very troubled."

My mother, voice shaking, said, "When we told him about the move, he said he didn't want to go. He wanted to stay with you."

My father, clearly struggling, took her hand and looked at the others. Then, crouching down in front of me, eyes moist but steady, he asked, "George, in two days we're going to America. We need to know what you want to do. Stay with Ahne and Ähni? Or go with us?"

I sobbed harder. My voice came in pieces through the tears. "Papa… I… don't… know… where… I… belong," I said and then collapsed into uncontrollable sobs.

The room went still. All of them—my parents, Ahne, Ähni—stood motionless, quietly crying. No one spoke. The weight of the moment pressed down on all of us.

Papa tried again. He said softly, "We need to know, son."

I whispered through gritted emotion, "Papa... I don't know. I don't know! I feel all alone!"

Ahne knelt again and took my hand. Her voice shook as she said, "George, just do what's in your heart. Trust what's in your heart."

My voice cracked as I said, "Ahne, I don't know what's in my heart. It's all messed up."

I looked back and forth from my parents to my grandparents. There was a long pause. And then I heard it. No one spoke, but I heard a voice. Not from the room but from somewhere deeper. "You are not alone," the voice said.

In that instant, the mist lifted. The weight broke. I could breathe. I turned to my father and still crying said, "Papa."

He looked up. "What, son?"

"I'll . . ." I hesitated, trembling. "I'll go with you."

And then I collapsed again, sobbing. But this time it was a release.

The adults looked at each other through tears that flowed, and finally, slowly they surrounded me. They embraced each other like survivors, clinging to what remained after a shipwreck.

I didn't feel brave. I didn't feel strong. I had long seen myself as weak. And I was. But what I felt then, unexpected and quiet, was a sense of peace. Not at peace with the decision. There was no peace in that. No matter what I chose something precious would be lost and missed. But peace in the moment. Peace in letting go.

Was it the best decision? The right one?

That could not be known then. Destiny would have to answer that at another time.

COMING TO AMERICA

The day of departure came quickly after that. Surprisingly, the lead-up to it was not as difficult as I expected. The drama and real difficulty came two days earlier at Ahne's house. Once I changed my mind, I didn't have much time to reconsider my decision. The need to catch up and pack what I would take to the New World helped keep me focused and engaged in my thoughts.

But on the morning of D-Day, anxiety and regret swept over me like a storm rolling down the Erms Tal. The dread of saying goodbye to grandparents, aunts, and uncles paralyzed me. Yet nothing weighed heavier than parting from Ahne.

The true heartbreak came at her doorway. She tried to be strong, but her eyes betrayed her long before her lips did. When she pulled me into her arms, I felt her whole body tremble with the force of what she couldn't say. The scent of her apron, the warmth of her embrace—those simple things branded themselves into me deeper than any words of blessing. When I finally stepped away, she pressed a crumpled, tear-stained handkerchief into my palm, as if she was giving me something of hers that would send her presence with me. I walked away with her silent tears still clinging to my shoulder, knowing that both of us were leaving pieces of our hearts on that threshold.

As expected, that was not easy, but it didn't drag on for long either. I cried for a long time on the train to Bremerhaven, which took much of the day. When we got to the ship dock, I saw the USS *General W. G. Haan*, and the tears stopped. The numbness began to wear off, and I was feeling emotionally stable again. Perspective was everything.

A six-year-old who had lived a sheltered life hundreds of miles from the coast and had never even seen so much as a lake, much less a small boat was standing at the base of a 523-foot World War II battleship's boarding ramp. Ships and small boats were missing in Ahne's *Märchen*. Unknowns.

Apprehension, sorrow, and fear gave way to curiosity and bemusement. All I could think of was, *Wow, we are going on that!? What is that going to be like?*

I could not imagine, but I didn't have to wait long to find out.

As I ascended the ramp with my parents and brothers trailing behind, curiosity began to swirl into excitement, emerging as a flicker of hope amid the turmoil that had brought me to this place. Yet beneath the vibrant facade of new experiences and unfamiliar surroundings, an ache pulsed in my heart—a stark reminder of the chaos I suppressed inside. The bittersweet realization washed over me. I could feel a glimmer of belonging alongside my family, but it was overshadowed by the weight of my silent anguish, each step echoing the haunting intensity of my inner pain.

After we checked into our small room in the ship's hull, it didn't take long for my father, Wolfgang, and me to go topside. As the moment of the ship's departure approached, I was filled with anticipation and excitement. I found myself hugging the railings on the main deck.

It wouldn't be long until I found out what this was going to be like! Oh, boy!

With a thunderous blast from the ship's horn, the massive ship surged forward, separating from its mooring, charting its course into the open sea. As the dock shrank into the distance, swallowed by the horizon, a disquieting emptiness settled in my chest. Sailing farther from

Germany's coastline, each passing wave was a reminder of what I was leaving behind. With every mile we drifted, the sadness returned, relentless and suffocating. The vastness of the North Sea mirrored the aching void inside me.

The ingredients of an adventure filled with drama were all there: a young, scared, sheltered boy on a big ship crossing a big ocean in the middle of winter. Neither he nor his family had any idea of the stakes involved in this venture. I had just experienced the two most chaotic and painful days of my life. *How much more drama could I take? How would things turn out for me?* The answers to that question would have to wait. The way things were shaping up at the beginning of the eight-day Atlantic crossing did not look promising.

Once in the North Sea, the ship soon left behind the mainland of Germany and the only life I had known and entered the 350-mile-long English Channel. Initially, the sight of any land mass disappeared. Gradually, the mainland of two other countries appeared. On the starboard side was the coast of England, on the port side, the coast of France.

Spellbound, Wolfgang and I were fascinated with our experience on the main deck, initially intrigued by new sights, sounds, and smells. The acrid, pervasive smell of salt water in the air was vastly different from the clear air I was used to breathing. The rhythmic waves coming at the ship were mesmerizing. They had a hypnotic effect on me, numbing my pain.

It did not take long, especially for this six-year-old, to figure out why they were called waves. The ship would slice through these churning, agitated waters like a surgeon's scalpel. My brother and I were both baffled by this spectacle, which went as far as the eye could see. Where did all these waves come from? What was making them so agitated?

Although it was winter, it was not bitterly cold as the water's maritime effect made it bearable to be on the deck for several hours without being chilled to the bone. Wolfgang and I spent much of the first full day of the journey on the lower deck, taking it all in.

Initially, it was an amazing experience, which captivated our attention. We couldn't get enough of it. But that would change profoundly.

It did not take long for the ship to navigate the English Channel and leave behind a lot of things. Not only had we left Germany, but the mainland of France and England had suddenly disappeared behind us. That meant we were leaving the continent of Europe and entering open waters. We set our sights on America as we entered the Atlantic, though it would be several days before we would see land again.

In the open water, one of the first differences that struck us was the staggering size of the waves. The transformation was nothing short of breathtaking. Swells rose like watery mountains ready to collapse. These winter swells propelled our massive battleship around like a mere cork in a tempest. The ship would ascend one of these sizable swells as it grew taller only to slide down into deep troughs as the wave passed. The ship rose and plunged into another swell as a heart-stopping warning shot through me, whispering, *This could be it*. After a prolonged period of endless repeating swells, I chose to retreat to the *safety* of the ship's hold.

Not surprisingly, the ship's deck was vacant of people except for one moment when Papa took us up from the hold to show us what the uncontrollable fury of nature looked like. Neither of us felt the need to be that terrified again, so we crossed that off our list. After that, on the captain's orders, no one was allowed on the deck. It was that dangerous. That meant the entire family was sequestered in our small cabin in the hold of the ship for the next seven days.

The naive, innocent questions like "Where are all these waves coming from?" were replaced by more important questions like "Are we going to die? Is our ship going to sink? Does this captain know what he is doing?" We had now entered the survival phase.

The lead-up to this fateful voyage had taken a toll on me, but it could not come close to the debilitating week-long sickness that I and the rest of the family endured. The frightful, constant undulating motion of the ship created a peril that put us in a state of survival.

Persistent vomiting replaced eating as our appetite for food was lost at sea for several days. It felt like drowning in slow motion—no escape, just the fear that this wouldn't end well. If someone had warned my family about the rough February ship crossing of the Atlantic Ocean, my difficult decision would have been easy; I would have stayed in Germany, along with the rest of the family.

It seems like all good, or in our case horrible, things come to an end. Days later, the waves started to get smaller as we approached the shallower waters near the shores of America. Most of us started to feel better as the motion was no longer a constant thrill, or threat depending on how you looked at it, on the eight-day monster aquatic rollercoaster.

When the captain called out that land was visible off the starboard bow, Wolfgang and I finally summoned the strength to return to the deck. It had been days since we dared venture above, but the promise of America pulled us like a lifeline. There, through the haze, we caught our first glimpse of the New World. A ragged coastline, dark and beckoning, stretched along the horizon. But the deck no longer felt like a place of wonder. What had once thrilled us now felt haunted. We stood not as adventurers but as survivors. The sea had turned cruel, and the journey had stripped away the romance of ocean travel. The salt air still clung to everything, but now it carried the scent of fear, not freedom. We had braved a gauntlet of storm and sickness, and every inch of our crossing had come at a cost.

To set foot on this strange shore felt less like a new beginning and more like staggering off a battlefield—shaken, grateful, and forever changed. The weariness of our exhausting ordeal was overcome when we passed the face of Lady Libertas, the Roman goddess of freedom. She smiled down on us as our ship passed under her vigilant eye and the torch that she held out to the "tired, poor, huddled masses yearning to breathe free," as the words etched into the lady's pedestal declared. Someone should have added the "sickly, poor huddled masses yearning to breathe without throwing up."

When we disembarked from our ship, we were all overcome with emotions that had been bottled up from before we even started this tempestuous trip. My emotions churned in silence. Relief washed over me now that the brutal ocean crossing was behind us, but it came laced with something heavier. The pain of separation still clung to me like wet clothes, impossible to shake. I made a quiet vow: I'd bury the life I left behind and pretend it didn't matter. It was the only way to survive. Facing it head-on would tear me apart. Denial was a kind of mercy.

Only when the fear, grief, and relief settled into their proper bins could I begin to face whatever this new world might hold. Stepping into this land, I felt it in my bones. I was a stranger in a strange place.

As I paused to process what I was experiencing, my mind traveled back to a three-thousand-year-old story. The book of Ruth was one of Ahne's favorite stories in the Bible. When Ruth and her mother-in-law, Naomi, were both widowed, Ruth left her family and traveled with Naomi back to her homeland. I now knew what a burden it must have been for Ruth to tell Naomi, "Your people will be my people, your God my God" before she departed on her journey. After Ruth arrived in the strange land, feeling like a stranger, she assimilated so well that she ended up in the bloodline of Jesus, the Messiah.

I wasn't expecting to assimilate into anyone's bloodline, but upon arrival, I could wholeheartedly identify with what it was like to be a stranger in a strange land, especially when we entered the world's largest city to visit the world's largest train station. It took me years to deal with and overcome that trauma.

At that time, America's borders were closed to immigration. To be allowed into the country required special approval by the US Congress, which my family had obtained. The historic Ellis Island, where millions of immigrants coming to America were processed, was closed. We were processed at New York's Grand Central Station, where I felt like an ant. Our family may have been the only immigrants on board the ship who were processed.

All around us were massive skyscrapers that rose from the ground like grass in Ähni's *Weise*. Bewildered, I had never seen anything like this.

So, this is America? Is everything here this big? And what is it with the people here? I wondered. *Everyone is in such a rush to get somewhere. Where are they all going in such a big hurry?*

Wait a minute. "Where are we going?" I asked my mother.

"Minnesota," she told me.

That was where her sister lived. *Where is that?* I thought. *What is in store for me next? What is my life going to be like?* I was overwhelmed with so many questions, thoughts, and fears that I shut down and went along like a robot, blindly following without a fuss.

We made our way from the shipping dock to the station and caught a train to Minnesota. I realized we were in another world, one that bore little resemblance to the world I had left. Once we got on the train, however, the minute my head hit the pillow in the sleeper car, I was out like a light. I was exhausted and emotionally drained.

This weeklong journey had taken a toll on me. For the first time in a long time, I slept well as the train rumbled on its rails to our new home.

A NEW HOME

The train rumbled through big cities, small towns, and even quaint villages that caught my attention. We traveled across rivers and through countrysides with fields of stubble and dense forests. We changed trains and traveled farther into the heartland of America.

When we finally reached our destination, Duluth, Minnesota, the sun had set. It was dark again. Greeting us when we got off the train was a blast of frigid air that made me ask in frustration, "Where are we?"

My aunt and uncle, whom I had never known or met, greeted us and took us to their car. We all squeezed into a Chevy station wagon for an hour-long drive along the dark shore of the world's largest freshwater lake. A bright moon lit up the frozen shore of Lake Superior as we drove along Highway 61 to my new hometown of Silver Bay.

SILVER BAY, TACONITE CAPITAL OF THE WORLD

When we arrived in Silver Bay in 1957 it was a town carved out of wilderness only a few years earlier. Every house was less than two miles from Lake Superior as the crow flies. Reserve Mining Company, formed by two large steel companies in the East, was responsible not only for establishing this town but also for building it from the ground up.

Most of the houses in this town of four thousand had been built within the previous three years. Reserve Mining Company, known locally as just Reserve, was built as a state-of-the-art taconite processing plant right on the shore of Lake Superior.

Taconite, a low-grade iron-bearing rock, was mined on the iron ranges of northeastern Minnesota. Trains brought railcars loaded with iron ore from the open-pit mines fifty miles inland to the plant at Silver Bay. The primary function of the plant was to process the iron ore, which included crushing the rough rock into a substance resembling dark gray flour. A magnetic separator process isolated the iron component from the crushed ore. The powder sediment that was left was effused into the lake by an artificial river originating from the plant.

The iron component, representing about a quarter of the original ore, was further processed for shipment to the steel mills. Since it was not possible to ship the iron as dust, it had to be shaped and hardened into pellets that were slightly larger than peas. This was done in the pelletizer division of the plant, which was a room with machinery that rolled the iron dust into pellets hardened in furnaces. In that part of the plant everything was covered with a persistent coating of black iron dust.

When we arrived, the plant was expanding its operations, producing billions of iron pellets that were loaded onto a fleet of visiting ore carriers, which transported their loads of iron across the Great Lakes to the steel mills in the East.

One of these vessels stood out to me: the *Edmund Fitzgerald*. I had the opportunity to see it being loaded at Reserve's dock on two occasions. In its day it frequently visited the plant and was famous for being the largest iron ore carrier on the Great Lakes. However, it achieved international recognition when "the winds of November came early," and it sank in 1976.

The amount of iron that these carriers transported from the plant to the iron-hungry steel mills put Silver

Bay on the map as the Taconite Capital of the World in the 1960s. To meet this demand, the plant had to scale up production, which created an urgency to hire skilled workers like my father. It was because of the plant's need for labor, specifically electricians, that my father left his family and native Germany to move forty-six hundred miles for a job that was offered to him. It is likely that his skills as an electrician combined with the immediate need for electricians by the plant had a major influence on the congressional approval of our family's immigration.

My aunt had told my mother about this job in letters. She passed the information on to my father, who was not only intrigued but also bold and brave enough to uproot his young family for an unknown job in an unknown country. This has always been the official reason given why my father made this life-altering move. There were also unconfirmed rumors that my aunt embellished her letters with reports of how the streets in America were lined with gold. If that had been true, it would not have caused any harm. However, we quickly discovered that these were only rumors.

There was one big caveat in the plan that brought our family to America. My father didn't speak English. When he arrived, the mining company that had recruited him—

job guaranteed, no interview needed, officially vetted by Congress—turned him away at the door.

What!? He couldn't believe it, but as an electrician in a plant full of high-voltage equipment, conveyor belts, and industrial machinery, communication wasn't a perk; it was a matter of life and death. And someone had forgotten to mention that Papa didn't speak English. Fortunately, the job was still his . . . in theory. But safety came first. He was told to go learn English. It wasn't a no. It was a not yet.

Our family of five was stranded in the middle of Minnesota with no income, no support, and a debt equivalent to $100,000 in today's dollars from our transatlantic move. Everything we owned could have fitted in a grocery cart. There would have even been room for the coats on our backs, which were not heavy enough for the cold northern Minnesota winter.

It would be easy to criticize the company. But looking back, they made the right call. This wasn't cruelty. It was common sense. And even more importantly, my father didn't see himself as a victim. This is not a story about social justice or grievances or what someone deserved. Wrongs were done, and they play a key role in this story. But this isn't a tale of victims seeking justice or compensation. It's a story about overcomers. It is about people who meet challenges head-on. Who stood their ground, stretched, endured, failed, tried again, and in their darkest hours leaned on something greater than themselves. For us, that meant trusting in God and trusting that the road ahead would make sense in time.

If you asked my father, he wouldn't have said he was wronged. He would've said, "I have a problem. I need to fix it." That's how problems were approached then. There were no forms to fill out. No committees to petition. No writers that produced think pieces or hot takes to elevate public awareness or opinion. The formula was simple:

Step 1: Identify the problem. (He couldn't speak English.)

Step 2: Fix it. (Learn English.)

It wasn't glamorous, and it wasn't easy. But it was clear. And that clarity gave him purpose and dignity.

Sometimes I imagine how the same situation might unfold today. It's tempting to speculate: public outcry, legal challenges, even legislation mandating multilingual signage in industrial workplaces. The narrative might frame my father as an example of systemic injustice, a man thrown out into the cold by an uncaring system.

But that's not how he saw it. And it's not how we lived it.

There were no protest signs. No media coverage. Just a man with a family and a problem to solve.

It's worth noting something that would go unnoticed today. His employment wasn't denied. It was deferred. And the expectation was that he would meet the standard, not that the standard would be lowered for him. There were no free English classes. No programs or subsidies. He found a way. He had to. And when he could speak enough English to work safely, he was hired just as promised.

And in the meantime? He swept floors at the local school to provide for his family. That was the help we were given—a door that wasn't closed but also wasn't wide open. The rest was up to us. Had all the social programs that exist today been available in the 1950s, our story would have been diminished by dependence.

Looking back, I realize how that moment shaped my family. It taught us that help doesn't always come in the form of handouts or policy. Sometimes it looks like a high bar and a quiet vote of confidence: "You can meet it. We believe in you."

My father never forgot that. Neither did I.

At the time, I didn't fully understand the weight of what he'd carried. But as I faced my struggles—challenges, failures, inner trauma—I realized I was following a path he had quietly carved.

I fought through adversity not just for my own sake, but because I didn't want him to see how hard it was for me. Not because I feared his judgment, but because I revered his sacrifice. Because if he saw me faltering, I feared he might second-guess his decision to uproot our family, to chase the promise of a new land with no guarantees.

His courage became my compass. And though we never spoke those words aloud, I carried his example like a torch through every storm.

Our family's story of immigration and my father's legacy can be summed up as one generation choosing risk and responsibility so the next one can choose to endure, overcome, and carry it forward.

ASSIMILATION

We stayed with my aunt, uncle, and three cousins for several months. Their new home was comfortable but small. It became even smaller when we moved in, doubling the number of occupants to ten. However, I was accustomed to living in space-challenged quarters.

Confinement had reached new levels on the trip to America. The ship's cabin, where we were all held for several days, was smaller than my room in the house my parents rented in Dettingen. The train ride halfway across America and the crowded car ride up the shore were both so confining that they would make sardines blush.

Somehow, it didn't bother me much to live in this small house with four adults and six children. Perhaps it was because I was still a child and small and didn't require a lot of space. Or I had been conditioned to not require space. The only time I experienced the freedom of open spaces was when I played in Ähni's *Wiese*.

When we arrived in Silver Bay, everyone believed enrolling me in school was the best way for me to assimilate—everyone, that is, except me. My brothers were exempt from such merciless thinking as they were too young. My having cold feet about school wasn't just from the bitter winter. It was rooted in two deep fears: fear of the unknown and fear of people.

I don't recall having those fears in my medieval village, where I'd faced panthers and dragons. I suspect I picked them up on the journey. Butterflies danced in my stomach as we boarded the battleship to America, paired with a tight-lipped apprehension about the unknown. But those butterflies morphed into terror when the Atlantic's big waves hit us.

The fear of people showed up when we arrived. And where better to develop that fear than in the suffocating crowd of New York City strangers nearly running me over? That kind of threat had no counterpart in the friendly village where I grew up.

In my past life, I was a happy-go-lucky kid. But this was a different culture. I could no longer blend in—or hide—as I had before. And fearful that I'd have nowhere to hide, I fought the idea of going to school. As far as I was concerned, we could delay that indefinitely.

When my aunt and my parents met with the school principal, I lost that battle. They decided I would start kindergarten. It was winter, and the school year was already halfway over. I had completed a year of kindergarten in Germany and should have been in first grade, but they thought it better for me to repeat kindergarten. So that's what I did.

If there were such a thing as a fear meter, mine would've exploded when they took me to school that first day. I met the principal, Mr. Davis, who told me how excited he was to welcome me. But as he led me down the hallway, I wasn't feeling any of his excitement.

We stopped at a closed classroom door. Mr. Davis got the teacher's attention, and when Mrs. Miller came to the door, the two of them talked. I couldn't hear or understand what they were saying, but I had a fairly good idea what the topic was.

After their conversation, Mr. Davis introduced me. Mrs. Miller shook my hand and gave me a warm hug that—for one second—put me at ease. That second vanished quickly as the three of us walked into a classroom of thirteen boys and girls, all of their eyes locked in on me. I wasn't just the new kid. I looked different and felt out of place, too.

Where are these adults taking me? I thought. *Oh, the front of the class! No problem. It's perfectly okay to put me up in front of this group. I'll get over it.*

"Or not," I added silently, as I fidgeted behind the two sets of legs that offered some cover. Peering out from behind them, twenty-six eyes stared back at me. I felt more uncomfortable than when I'd faced the black panthers and dragons in my vivid dream. I was not ready for show-and-tell or anything that made me the center of attention. This was showtime, and I hadn't rehearsed.

When Mr. Davis left, it was just me and Mrs. Miller standing in front of the class. I now had receipts for why this whole school idea was a bad one. Before exiting, Mr. Davis paused to ensure me everything would work out. Mrs. Miller began to introduce me.

Looking down at me squirming behind her, Mrs. Miller said, "Class, I'm sure you noticed someone new. He's come a long way to join us." She stooped down and smiled at me, frozen stiff, with my teeth about to chatter. "This is George, a brave boy who came here from Germany with his family. I want you all to welcome him as your new classmate."

She glanced around the room, then back at me. "Right now, he's a little nervous and upset because he doesn't know how nice you all are. So, class, guess what you're going to do?" A pause. A girl in the front row raised her hand. "Yes, Cindy, what do you think we should do to make him feel welcome?"

"We can show him how nice we are, Mrs. Miller!" Cindy beamed.

I didn't understand everything they were saying, but that did not stop me from feeling embarrassed. *Great! Is everything in America going to be this embarrassing?* I thought.

"Wonderful, Cindy!" Mrs. Miller exclaimed. "You're on the right track. Now, how do we demonstrate that to him? Does anyone have ideas?"

Another girl raised her hand and said, "We can invite him to play and share our toys."

"Another great answer, Judy!" Mrs. Miller said, beaming at me. "That reminds me of something. But I don't want to embarrass George."

Ahh. We are kind of late for that.

"I was told that when George's family left Germany, they could only bring so much. I'm sure they had to leave toys behind. Imagine how sad you'd feel if you left your home and relatives and couldn't bring your toys."

If they only knew how few toys I had or needed. Several girls looked stunned. All I could think was, *I brought my top. I'm good.*

"You all have more toys than you can play with, right?" Mrs. Miller asked. "George has very few. What if each of you brought in one toy you think he'd like? Would you miss it?" You could've heard a pin drop. Everyone hung on her words. Not understanding much of them, I fidgeted nervously behind her, but I was beginning to feel something shift. Mrs. Miller continued, "What if each of you brought a toy tomorrow that you think George would like? Could you do that?"

Before she even finished, a viral wave of excitement swept the class. For the first time, I almost smiled. Their reaction disarmed me. For a moment, I forgot myself. Kids jumped from their seats to shake my hand and hug me in an impromptu meet-and-greet. Mrs. Miller didn't stop them. She just smiled, satisfied. Out of the corner of my eye, I saw Mr. Davis still watching from the door, smiling. Then he left, no doubt pleased with how it turned out.

My parents were thrilled with the report of my first day. Of course, I downplayed it. No need to oversell this school thing. It was a marathon not a sprint. I couldn't expect every day to go that well. If nothing else, that first day grounded me. It also helped keep things in perspective during the hard days. If I made school sound too rosy, it would be harder to feel sorry for myself, which I was prone to do. I'd been through trauma, and I coped with it mostly by burying the pain.

Since I was the most surprised by how well the first day went, it's only fair to wonder *what will happen next.*

To no one's surprise, especially mine, it went very well. Why wouldn't it? I had Christmas in February. There were more than enough toys for me and my two younger brothers. I was humbled by the class's generosity. Even Mrs. Miller brought something. It was as many presents as I had received in all my first six Christmases combined. But since I didn't need or use many toys, one caught my attention: a toy six-shooter and holster. It was love at first sight.

I watched many Westerns at my aunt's house with my uncle and cousins. They were wildly popular in the 1950s. The cowboys, Indians, and horses—so different from the knights on their steeds and the dragons I had grown up with—fascinated me. They all shared a commonality. Except for Ähni's horse, I had never seen any of them in real life, on either side of the ocean. So, to me cowboys and Indians were mythical. And I had learned to think mythically, thanks to Ahne's many *Märchen* and *Geschichten.* Thinking mythically was my second language. English would be my third.

Watching those Westerns had primed me. That toy gun and holster triggered something deep. Proudly, I strapped it on. Beaming with a smile so wide it made my face hurt, all I could say to my new classmates was "Thank you" in my broken English and limited vocabulary.

That mythical toy gun and holster became a bridge between my old world and this new one. And, as you'll see, it opened a portal to the mythical world of Indian lore and the big lake, which I would soon meet.

ANOTHER HUMBLE BEGINNING

*M*y father worked as a school janitor for most of the months that we lived with my cousins. His English improved to the point that Reserve hired him. By fall, he was working at the plant, and we left the tight quarters of my aunt's house for different tight quarters.

Due to its labor needs, the plant hired laborers more quickly than houses could be built for them. To provide temporary housing, a trailer court was established near the plant and Lake Superior. My parents were able to acquire a "spacious" twenty-six-foot trailer that we called our home. If you lined up our trailer next to modern RVs families use for vacations today, it would look like a tugboat that greeted the battleship in the New York Harbor.

After moving in, one day my father came home with a major surprise. He drove up to our trailer in our first car. I was seven at the time. After my austere upbringing in the village, I was struck by how much Americans were dependent on cars. But I came to appreciate the amount of freedom it brought them. When available, freedom is not something you refuse or give up, especially if you want to be an American, which was the goal.

That car may have been a turning point. With eyes full of anticipation, I opened the door and settled into the faded upholstery of the blue 1954 Ford sedan as the afternoon sun cast a warm glow through its windshield. In that moment, nestled in the surroundings of what was starting to look like my humble new home and life, I marveled at how this new world seemed to shimmer with possibilities and new freedoms. *Maybe the streets are lined with gold in America*, I mused. That whimsical thought danced through my mind like the golden rays filtering through the windshield. It was more than just a car; it was a vessel of hope and dreams that ignited my spirit of exploration.

Considering my upbringing, not far removed from medieval times, it did not require many modern material possessions to influence and shape me. This made assimilation easier, especially when it was baked into the modern conveniences that were everywhere. One such example was the first "hi-tech" black-and-white television set. It came with a low-resolution, seventeen-inch cathode-ray tube screen. There was no remote control in those days. If you wanted to change the channel, you had to get up and turn the dial on the TV.

In the 1950s, America had just three networks that offered a rich array of programming, reflecting the wholesome values of the time. These shows became the gold standard for families aspiring to learn American culture and were a vital part of our journey toward assimilation. Our family of five spent countless hours in front of that television, which significantly improved our command of English. The programs aimed at younger audiences offered valuable life lessons. Each episode captivated us, instilling good character and values while keeping us entertained. We could hardly wait for the next installment, quickly forgetting everything else, including Ahne's *Geschichten*.

Our little TV was an invaluable resource. It served as a tutor, personal guide, and a comforting escape when life became overwhelming and difficult. That set also drew me into the mythical world of cowboys and Indians. Every time I watched a Western, I had my holster and trusty sidearm, locked and loaded, strapped to my side.

I cast myself as the guardian of my family by taking out the bad guy whenever he showed his face on the screen. That pistol was a cap gun.

The 1950s and 1960s was the golden era of cap guns, when kids like me were captivated by the Westerns, which dominated television programming. The caps came as small rolls of paper, about as wide as a pencil. The paper was dotted with dabs of gunpowder perfectly spaced. As the roll fed into the chamber, a powder dab aligned with the trigger strike point. When fired, the hammer struck the powder, producing a loud bang that mimicked the sound of real gunfire.

But the real magic happened after, as the gunpowder smoke lingered, its intoxicating fragrance prompted an instinctive reaction. I would proudly raise the gun to my pursed lips, blow across the barrel before thrusting the gun into my holster with a satisfying flourish. For a minute, I thought I was John Wayne. I transitioned from a boy to a defender to a guardian to a man many times when I was packing heat. Who knew cap guns could be responsible for such a sudden maturation in boys?

Since guns, even toy ones, are controversial today, it should be noted that there is no evidence that toy guns were responsible for someone growing up to become a mass murderer with an "assault" weapon. In the 1950s and 1960s, mass murder was something foreign. We never heard about it because it didn't happen. Every boy watched numerous Westerns with countless gunfights. Toy cap guns were as common for boys as Barbie dolls were for girls.

The tiny trailer marked the beginning of my second humble beginning. The car represented freedom to limitless exploration. The TV represented a portal to a new world of fantasy and imagination. Where are the problems here?

For those, I must circle back to the trailer and an incident that happened there. This is a poignant example of what life inside was like for the five of us, as well as illustrating the cramped nature of our living conditions. It also shows how passionate I became about the fantasy world of cowboys and Indians.

Our living area was a combination kitchen, dining area, and living room, all in close quarters. One evening, I was playing a game of cowboys and Indians in the living room with Wolfgang. He was next to the TV at one end of the living room. I was getting ready to lasso him from the kitchen area, where my mother had a pot of boiling water on the stove. To give this perspective, the lasso was made from a twelve-foot rope. With it I could have lassoed my brother, who was on the other side of the living area.

After I waved my lasso over my head, I reached back and was ready to toss the rope around my brother's neck. But unbeknownst to me, the loop of the lasso had roped the pot of boiling water. When I thrust the rope forward with a crisp yank, I pulled the pot off the stove, drenching my right leg with boiling water. In pain, I immediately collapsed to the floor with third-degree burns. I was bedridden for five weeks as my leg healed. It was a painful experience to say the least, especially when my mother changed the dressing. But once healed, this cowboy was ready to get back on his horse for more adventure.

When I finally recovered from this terrifying experience, Papa would have another surprise for the family.

GITCHE GUMEE

One sun-drenched afternoon, driven by an adventurous spirit, I ventured down a path through the woods. As I followed the winding trail, a sense of anticipation danced within me as though I was being beckoned by nature. Suddenly, the woods surrendered to an expansive clearing, and there before me lay the largest freshwater lake in the world, shimmering under the golden rays of the sun. Its beauty was so pristine it took my breath away.

This moment marked the dawn of many encounters with the majestic waters that the Native Americans revered as Gitche Gumee. My heart raced, unburdened by the haunting memories of a turbulent ocean crossing that should have instilled a lifetime of fear of deep waters. Instead, as I stood there, a small boy dwarfed by the vastness before me, I was struck by an indescribable connection, a strange sense of belonging to this majestic body of water.

The enormous atmosphere of Lake Superior overwhelmed me. A beach of warm, soft sand invited me closer to the water's edge. The gentle waves offered soothing melodies that seemed to echo through my very soul. It was as if this lake transcended the very essence of what I had known.

Gone were the tales of knights and castles from the idyllic world I had left. They were replaced by the disquieting allure of the unexplored realm lying before me. I gazed out over this liquid canvas, and as far as the eye could see, the sky and water blended seamlessly. An undeniable magnetism gripped my heart as this bewitching lake murmured promises of forgotten secrets and untold adventures. Enchanted, I stood on that shore as the gentle waves lapped at my bare feet, wrestling with feelings of awe and a fear of the unknown.

In that moment of stillness, I knew I was not just an observer but a part of a far greater story waiting to unfold in a new and different fairytale world. In the tapestry of my early life, I had suddenly become acutely aware of time's loom as it weaved together a history that was unknown to me. I was surrounded by it, and it grounded me.

Where I grew up, little had changed over the centuries; the boy in medieval times who once played with a top on the cobblestone streets seemed to echo within me as I had found joy in those simple pleasures of a simple life. While strolling along the beach, I took a deep breath of fresh air, allowing it to fill my lungs and uplift my spirit. It was as if all my concerns had vanished. The sensation of walking along the water's edge made me feel incredibly light, as if I could walk on the water itself, though I suspect the coldness of the water might prevent that. It was a natural high, a lifting of the spirit that many seek through drugs, power, or adrenaline rushes. For me, it was simply a walk to this special beach, one I would return to often.

The second time I visited the lake, I felt a strange peace. Ever since arriving in this new and unfamiliar country I had never heard of, I found myself drawn to the lake. Despite experiencing the traumatic events that left me feeling profoundly alone, even when surrounded by well-meaning adults, I never felt alone on this beach. Here, solitude did not isolate me; it embraced me.

At first, I didn't understand why. But during this second visit, something inside me began to settle. My thoughts were clear. My body, too, responded. I discovered agility and quickness that seemed to come from nowhere, skills that would serve me well in schoolyard games and sports later. With fresh breezes off the lake filling my lungs, running up and down the beach not only made me healthy but also strong and alive.

I began to speak to the lake, softly at first, as though to a friend who listens more with the heart than the ears. I felt a peace here that I had not known elsewhere. This beach seemed to resonate at a different frequency, a purity that bypassed my busy thoughts and found its way directly into my soul. Though I was alone, I was never lonely. There was no fear—only a quiet serenity, a gentle welcome that whispered, *You belong here.* It was as though the lake had been waiting for me, and I for it.

In that stillness, I found myself to be something of a conduit—open, receptive, strangely attuned to something greater than myself. Thoughts came that didn't feel entirely my own, as if planted gently by a force that knew me better than I knew myself.

The everyday concerns of this strange new world were silenced by nature's simplicity: rocks, sky, water, and trees. I was the only sign of human life, yet I never felt out of place. The sun gleamed on the water's surface, scattering diamonds across the lake like a message just for me. In those glimmering waves, I found a strange sense of elevation, a lightness, as though I were ascending from the troubles of my young heart into a higher realm where nothing was lost, only remembered.

Perhaps I had known this place before, at another time. Was I being groomed for something? The thought didn't seem absurd here. Time itself felt different; centuries collapsed into seconds, as though the lake held memories far older than the land around it. This mystery compelled me. I began to wonder what lore might exist here, what stories of magic and morality. Would I find dragons here, too, hiding beneath the waves? Could another boy, hundreds or even a thousand years before me, have stood in this same place, seeking solace and discovering peace? The thought comforted me, as if my presence here was part of something timeless, ancient, and enduring. No answers came that day, only a deeper longing to return.

Several days passed, and with them came the unsettled feelings of change—the move, the new people, the disorientation of life in a trailer near a lake—I was just beginning to understand. When it all became too much, I knew exactly where I needed to be.

Back at my beach.

During the third visit to the lake, as I walked the familiar shoreline, I noticed something new. A smooth, beautiful piece of driftwood shaped and polished by the waves over time, lay nestled in the sand. Near it, a mangled, rusted can sat like an intruder on this sacred ground. I picked it up, curious and a little offended. Why had the lake treated these two objects so differently?

It struck me. The lake had polished the driftwood with tenderness but punished the metal can. Could the lake possess its own moral compass? Could it *discern* what belonged and what defiled? The idea both thrilled and humbled me.

The lake was more than a body of water. It was a force of good, a guardian of balance, rewarding harmony and punishing carelessness. It made me think about myself—how the lake had never once rejected me. Each visit had lifted my spirit. I arrived burdened but left lighter, more whole. Could it be that the lake treated me with kindness because it sensed something in me? Something good?

The idea filled me with quiet gratitude. Just maybe I was worthy of this friendship. The lake reminded me of Ahne—my beloved grandmother—who used to look at me with warmth and knowing after telling me a story. And wouldn't you know, each time I visited the lake, the sun would shine in just the same way, casting golden light across the waves like a smile from someone who loved me.

Moved by my feelings, I decided to act. I placed the rusty can on a fallen tree near the water, then stepped back about forty feet. With an ample supply of smooth stones at my feet, I began hurling them at the can. My aim was off at first, but I persevered. After what felt like dozens of throws, I struck it clean. The can went flying, tumbling into the underbrush, where it could no longer stain this sacred place. It felt good—not just because of the success of the throw, but the justice of it. I had defended the lake, and in doing so, it felt like I had honored something ancient and pure.

What I didn't realize then was that this small act of play would sharpen my aim and coordination for sports I had never heard of before—baseball, football, basketball. In some strange way, the lake had not only accepted me—it had trained me.

That night, I returned home full not only of peace, but of purpose. I wasn't just *visiting* the lake anymore. I belonged to it.

A NAME CAST WITH STONE

After my leg healed my dad announced, "We are moving again." This time it was to our new house in Silver Bay. After being bedridden for weeks, I shed no tears when we left the trailer two months later.

By this time, Papa worked regular shifts with a crew of electricians at the plant. Although he rarely expressed it, he felt both proud and grateful after arriving in this country. He had silently endured the disappointment and hardship of a job deferred, following a perilous journey across the Atlantic Ocean. At that point, he had no income and an $8,000 debt to cover his relocation expenses. Now, less than two years later, with the loan repaid, he was moving into his first house, supported by his wages of $2.90 per hour. Although he faced many challenges along the way, my father met them head-on and took them in stride. He believed that America's streets were lined with gold.

Going from no income to earning $2.90 per hour might not be a classic rags-to-riches tale, and viewed with amusement today, but in 1959 the results were undeniable. It laid the foundation for the successful assimilation of the entire family, currently spanning five generations.

I was thrilled to learn that I would have my own room for the first time. After we moved into the house on Horn Boulevard, I quickly settled into *my* new room. It did not take long for me to learn the language, lose my accent, and embrace the culture of my new friends. I no longer stood out, although I was not attempting to conceal anything. There were occasions, however, when it was almost necessary to keep my past private to avoid potential embarrassment or to draw unwanted attention. I never enjoyed being the center of attention. However, there was a notable exception to that. As I succeeded in sports and became more confident, I wanted to be the one with the ball. I wanted to make the play.

Most situations that prompted me to conceal my heritage were innocuous and harmless. There was one incident that was not. Shortly after we moved into our house, Wolfgang, Gerhard, and I were playing beside our metal garage near the neighbor's yard. We knew two older teenage boys lived next door, though we hadn't met them yet.

We were quietly immersed in our game, scooping dirt with our yellow Tonka dump truck, when the back door of the neighbor's house creaked open. We didn't notice until two shadows stretched across the gravel.

Chuck and John emerged.

John had slicked-back dark hair and a wiry frame. Chuck was heavier, with a messy mop of greasy brown hair. Both stared at us, their eyes already full of something sharp and mean.

"There they are!" Chuck exclaimed, his voice bubbling with enthusiasm.

"Told you they'd be out here," John replied matter-of-factly.

Startled, I looked up as they walked toward us. "Hi."

"You're the ones who just moved here from Germany?" Chuck asked.

"What?" I replied in a half whisper.

"Chuck, maybe they don't speak English," John replied sarcastically. "Or maybe they're just too good to talk to us. Hitler taught those Nazis that they were the *superior* race."

"Hey, Nazis, you... speakie... English?" Chuck responded in a mocking tone.

We didn't answer.

"Too good to answer, huh?" John asked. "Think you're better than us? Got a name, Nazi?"

Still nothing.

"How 'bout we give him a name," Chuck responded in a serious tone. "I got one. Let's call him *Superior*."

They cracked up laughing so hard they staggered.

Wolfgang clutched my arm and whispered, "I don't like them. They're mean."

"Hey, Chuck, did you hear that?" John asked as he recovered his balance. "The middle one spoke. What'd you say, squirt?"

"He said you're mean!" I yelled.

"Ohhh, looks like *Superior* speaks after all," John replied mockingly.

"Well, I'll be. Didn't see that comin'," Chuck added.

They stepped closer. Gerhard began to cry. "I want Mama!" he burst out emotionally.

"Aw, look at that. Baby Nazi's crying," John replied mockingly.

"George, let's run!" Wolfgang shouted.

I shook my head, still fiddling with the truck. "No," I said quietly. "If we run, they'll chase us. Just ignore 'em."

"What're they sayin'?" Chuck asked angrily.

John stooped down, picked up a few rocks, testing their weight in his palm. "Probably talkin' German. Sayin' how mean we are," he replied.

"Why don't you just leave us alone?" I demanded.

John grinned and said, "Whoa! Look out, Chuck. *Superior's* gettin' saucy."

"I've had enough of these snibblin' Krauts," Chuck said repulsively. "Let's show 'em how Americans welcome Nazis."

John handed a rock to Chuck.

"RUN!" I shouted.

A rock hissed past my ear like a hornet. It slammed into the metal garage wall behind me with a loud thud. It rang like a warning bell. I froze. Then another one crashed near Wolfgang's leg. That's when we ran.

Mother heard the commotion. When we reached the porch, she was already there. She pulled us inside and slammed the door shut behind us. We stood in the entryway, panting, crying, shaking.

"What happened?! Why are you crying?" our mother asked.

"The . . . neighbor . . . boys . . ." I answered between gasps. "They called us names; they threw rocks! One almost hit me in the head!"

"What?! What did you do?"

"We didn't do anything!" I replied angrily.

"We were just playing, and they came out and started yelling, calling us Krauts, Nazis," Wolfgang responded emotionally.

"Mama! I'm scared!" Gerhard sobbed.

She gathered him in her arms. "It's OK. You're safe now," she responded.

"Mama, why do those boys hate us?" I asked.

She paused. Her eyes darkened. "Maybe because we moved here from another country?" she offered.

"But that's not a reason to hate someone! I'm scared to go outside now," Wolfgang replied angrily.

"Me too, Mama," added Gerhard.

"I know. It'll get better."

"Mama, what's a Nazi? Are we . . . Are we Nazis?" Wolfgang asked.

Her face stiffened. She set Gerhard down gently and looked away. "Dear God, I didn't expect this," she said softly and then paused. "You'll have to ask your father when he comes home."

"Why? Is it something bad?" I asked. "Is everyone in this town going to hate us, too?"

I couldn't understand this reaction to our family just because my parents grew up in a time when Germany was at war. Neither of my parents had anything to do with it. For my mother and her family, it was so difficult that she couldn't even talk about it. She had risked her life escaping oppression that led to the death of her stepfather.

When Papa came home from work that evening, the matter was never discussed—not with us, anyway. Maybe Mama told him privately. Maybe they decided to protect us from knowing too much. We never heard any more about it. My parents stayed silent. So did we. I imagine they hoped ignorance could shield us better than understanding ever would, that if we didn't know too much, we wouldn't say the wrong thing.

Our family was having dinner several months later. By that time, we had grown to six, as Heidi, my sister, had been born. My mind went back to the altercation with the neighbor boys. It still bothered me. I frequently dwelt on it. Each time, I had more questions. That night at the dinner table, I was wrestling with some of those questions. Why did Papa want to leave his family in Germany and come to a place where people hated us? Wouldn't we have been better off there? What kind of country did we come to anyway where they treat people like that? What will happen to us here?

Disturbed by my thoughts, I got up from the table and went over to the sink. I turned on the faucet to fill my glass with water as I stared out the kitchen window into the darkness. There was one question that would haunt me for years: "Why did *I* come here?"

When I passed the gravy to Papa, I refrained from asking either of them those questions. It wasn't due to any fear. It just seemed practical to stay quiet. We all faced difficulties. I could not imagine how much greater my parents' challenges were compared to ours. They required much more time to master the language. I merely wanted to avoid burdening them with my questions and concerns.

Over many years, I found myself quietly pondering these questions. I found them challenging to resolve. Fortunately, I had my safe space where I could discuss and pose these questions as they emerged. Some came at me like stones being thrown. But the answers, those were harder to find—more like the ones I learned skipping stones across the lake, searching for calm in the ripples.

The move to our new home marked a period of accelerated change. I discovered my athletic self, taking up sports I had never played before. And Papa encouraged us to strive for academic excellence, making that a major focus.

I possessed an innate desire to learn, which stemmed from my inquisitive nature. When not in class, I would often participate in activities, such as playing on a field with new friends, using the gym, or spending time in the school library. I also developed new interests that occupied my remaining time. These new experiences and interests kept me actively engaged.

MISHIPIZHEU

My fascination with Native Americans began with the cap gun and holster from Mrs. Miller's kindergarten class. Like many boys my age, I was swept up in Westerns. But with no cowboys on the North Shore, my interest quickly shifted to those whose moccasins had truly tread on this land—the Chippewa Indians.

The Chippewa, also known as the Ojibwe, had a historical presence on the North Shore of Lake Superior. In a nearby town, there was an Indian burial ground. Whenever I found myself in the wilderness surrounding the town, I explored rock outcroppings, hoping to find hidden caves and discover Indian artifacts.

I spent large amounts of time in the library. In those days, decades before the advent of the Internet, information was available only in books, periodicals and reference books kept in schools and local libraries. I was passionate about resources related to Native American Indian traditions and nature crafts.

Two books stood out to me and revealed what I had missed—a connection not only to Indian folklore but also to the mythical medieval world that shaped my early years. From these books, I learned about the mythical creatures that appeared in my earlier dream, which ended with a voice saying: "You are not alone." I heard that message again when I faced the difficult decision that would decide my fate. Surprisingly, I never heard that voice on any of my visits to Lake Superior when I was alone. Maybe because I wasn't.

In the first book, *Book of Beasts: The Bestiary in the Medieval World*, the black panther was depicted as a star-speckled deity, exhaling a sweet fragrance and the only creature to inspire fear in dragons. This description both clarified and comforted me regarding the content of my dream.

The second was a dusty library book called *Native Legends of the Great Lakes and the Mississippi Valley*. I met the black panther's cousin: Mishipizheu. Different stories. Same eyes.

To the Ojibwe people he is real. They call him the underwater panther, a powerful and sacred being who lives beneath the lakes, guarding what lies below. He is both a feared and revered guardian and a punisher. He is known by many names—Mishipizheu, Mishibiji, Mishipeshu—and he always watches the waters.

Mishipizheu is no ordinary creature. Descriptions from Ojibwe elders and lore describe a massive feline body—like a panther or lynx—with scales of copper or horns covering its back, great curling horns rising from its head, and a tail that thrashes like a serpent. He stirs up storms with his presence. He hoards the sacred copper that lies beneath the lakebed. And he does not tolerate disrespect. Fishing in excess, mining the land without reverence, polluting the waters, littering the beaches, these are acts that awaken Mishipizheu's wrath.

There are stories of him sinking canoes, whipping up storms, and pulling offenders underwater without warning. But he is not malevolent. Like many spirits in Indigenous religions, Mishipizheu exists to maintain balance, to protect, and to guard.

He is closely tied to Lake Superior, which has swallowed more than its share of ships and secrets. If you've ever stood alone on its shoreline, as I have, when the clouds gather and the wind turns cold, you may have sensed it too—that feeling of something bigger, something ancient, just below the surface.

Although I did not know his name, I saw glimpses of him, felt his breath stir the grasses in dreams, and watched the water ripple where no wind blew. But it is essential to understand that Mishipizheu is not just an animal. He's not a symbol, not a metaphor. He is a spirit.

Mishipizheu is a force of nature, yes. But more than that, he reflects courage of conscience and the lake's voice. Once his presence is known, it cannot be unknown.

You don't summon Mishipizheu. He finds you. And when he does, everything changes.

You may not see him again, but if he sees you, the lake will speak.

PUFF THE MAGIC DRAGON

Silver Bay was as idyllic as Dettingen, but without a long history. Here, my family and the townsfolk were the pioneers, the first generation. It felt almost providential that I'd end up here, in a place that was unfamiliar yet strangely familiar. A new beginning. It was here, standing on the shore of Lake Superior, that I felt something deep inside me, like I was finally home. It felt as though I had been raptured out of my village into this unfamiliar town that I readily adopted as my own. Providing confirmation that I was in the right place was the overwhelming peace I felt standing on the shore of Lake Superior that first time.

Ahne had told me that all things work together for good for God's children. Initially, I couldn't see how that was possible, yet it proved to be accurate. For my thirteenth birthday, I received a Schwinn American Flyer bicycle and quickly appreciated its significance. It felt as though I had been given a magic carpet that opened hidden possibilities. The first led to freedom, and later, it opened a door to my very soul.

By this time, our family's adjustment and integration had progressed as well as we could have hoped for. There was still my unaddressed buried trauma of leaving Ahne. My many interests and activities masked it well—at least most of the time. When it became burdensome, my safe space was a thirty-minute bicycle ride away. I never needed an appointment either.

The rough places in my family's life were smoothed out like the rocks on my favorite shore. We were accepted in the community, and we did not stand out like when we first arrived. We started to be "normal" and assimilate. The earlier issue with our neighbor boys and the distress it caused did not recur. In fact, the situation was completely resolved, and we eventually became friends. They were responsible for the town's Independence Day fireworks display, to which they kindly invited both me and Wolf to help them. So, you could say that our relationship with them ended with fireworks.

These were the golden days of my adolescence in Silver Bay—memories lingered in my mind like the warm glow of a summer sunset. Those were times brimming with freedom, when my siblings and I, along with neighborhood kids, roamed our little corner of the world with an adventurous spirit. Each morning, we'd slip out of our houses as the sun was just beginning to rise, and we'd wander away until the dinner bell rang, or the evening stars began to twinkle in the sky.

Summer painted a canvas of daily escapades. Some days, the schoolyard became our kingdom, echoing with laughter and the cheers of impromptu baseball games that stretched until the golden hour. By that time, my stat line might read: 25 At Bats and 6 Home Runs. All the way home, my anticipation for tomorrow's slugfest would crescendo.

The next morning, the call of the wild might interrupt baseball. We would swap out our bats for fishing poles and embark on a two-mile hike through lush wilderness, our laughter mingling with the whispers of the trees. Our destination? Twin Lakes, a secret hidden gem where we would cast our lines in deep, sparkling waters, reeling in bass until our arms ached and our hearts brimmed with the joy of life's simple pleasures.

In the 1960s, Silver Bay was a slice of paradise for adolescent kids. In northern Minnesota, the winters tested our resilience with their bitter cold and snow, but in the summer, we thrived under a kind sun that provided sixteen hours of peak daylight, wrapping us in warmth and endless freedom.

Mornings unfolded with a sense of possibility and extended time to enjoy them. Parents trusted us to carve our own adventures. We scattered in different directions, some riding to the lake on their bikes, while others chose the thrill of casting our lines into the rivers that cradled our town. Those with licenses often felt the thrill of driving to the Baptism River, where time and worries were washed away in the falls draping the cool swimming hole.

Amidst the tapestry of these carefree days, parents felt a profound sense of ease. It was a time when we could return home just as the sun dipped below the horizon, and those fleeting moments weren't tainted with parental worries.

The close-knit fabric of our town also meant that tragedies, like the heartbreaking drowning of a teenager or a fall from lakeshore cliffs, cast shadows over those sun-drenched days. Such losses struck a heavy chord, reminding us all too vividly of life's fragility. But even in our grief, the rhythm of life would eventually guide us back, and the laughter would return to fill the air once more.

In a straight line, Lake Superior was a mere mile from our home, but by bicycle along the country roads, the distance was two or three miles. On one of these three-mile journeys, I found myself returning to my special shore on Lake Superior. Upon emerging from the wooded forest and reaching the rocky shore, I experienced the same emotions I had when I first discovered the lake's edge, feeling as though I had returned home after a prolonged absence.

It was a warm, sunny day. I dismounted my bicycle, allowing it to rest upon the rocks, and ran toward the peaceful, secluded shore that lay before me. The beach was adorned with smooth rocks of varying sizes. I began collecting some of the flatter rocks, filling my pockets until they were bulging and nearly overflowing. One by one, I retrieved the rocks from my pockets and skipped them across the lake. I dedicated the better part of an hour to this activity, exhausting my entire collection. Naturally, I replenished my supply several more times. It did not take long for me to devise a challenging game of seeing how many times my rocks would skip.

Just then, a seagull flew over my head and landed near me. While enjoying the skipping of stones across the water, my focus was captured by the island from which the seagull had appeared. It was adorned with steep cliffs and was about two hundred yards away. This observation presented yet another intriguing challenge. I had a strong arm from playing sandlot baseball all summer, but all my attempts to reach that island with a rock were futile. Riding my bike home later that day, my mind was captured by thoughts of how I could propel rocks dozens of yards farther than I was able to throw.

A week later, a bright sun and an azure, blue sky greeted me as I returned to the lake. The minute I reached the edge of the rock-lined shore, I jumped off the bike with excitement and ran to the water's edge. As I approached the waves lapping on the rocky shore, I pulled something from my back pocket.

That pesky island got the best of me last time and brought me back to earth. I had to face the fact that there was no way that I could throw a rock that far. While I may not have possessed any extraordinary abilities, I was fortunate enough to have my intellect, along with a powerful desire to overcome the challenges presented by that island. My sense of pride made it difficult for me to accept failure. I devised and prepared a battle plan for that island.

Having contemplated the challenge of launching a rock over such a distance for over a week, I devised a simple solution. Drawing inspiration from the classic

Sunday school story of David and Goliath, I felt inspired to attempt something similar. David's method of overcoming the giant involved a simple sling, a primitive weapon.

Never having seen one firsthand, I found the concept intriguing and worthy of investigation. After acquiring some rawhide and long leather thongs, I proceeded to construct one myself. Once completed, I was very eager to put it to the test. And so, here I was.

I carefully searched the shoreline, selecting suitable rocks to fill my pockets. Afterward, I retrieved the sling from my back pocket and began practicing with it. Initially, my attempts were not particularly successful, and I was grateful that no one was nearby, as they might have been at risk.

It required numerous practice throws to master the proper release, but I gradually improved as the rocks began to land in the intended direction. As my confidence grew, the rocks landed farther out in the water, coming increasingly closer to the island. Like Goliath, that island had no reason to be concerned when I produced my makeshift weapon. Much like David facing the giant, I imagine I appeared comical as well. Nevertheless, one should never underestimate a young man with a clear objective. That island was about to meet its match!

Eventually, one of the stones I propelled found its target, striking the island's cliff face and scattering rock and debris into the lake. After a subsequent throw that narrowly missed, I mounted my bicycle and returned home. The broad smile plastered on my face reflected a feeling of success and satisfaction.

But then things changed. I grew up and kept a busy schedule of junior high sports and academics. I excelled in both areas, ranking among the top athletes and scholars in my class. Sports, school, and new interests. The lake—once my refuge—faded into the background. I no longer made trips that once felt so important. All the rocks I had so lovingly skipped now lay forgotten, like the childhood dreams I left behind.

Not all the rocks on the beach were skipped. Some were collected and cherished. These were Lake Superior agates, which I kept in a glass jar in my room, a delightful reminder of past adventures.

My time at the library, which started with research into nature and Indigenous cultures, unexpectedly ignited a new interest and passion within me: science. I became enthusiastic and nerdy, eagerly anticipating the arrival of each new edition of *Scientific American* to read about the latest advancements. I especially looked forward to the latest science project of the month.

Going beyond simply reading about these projects, I constructed several of them from the magazine's plans. The more successful ones ended up as my project in the annual school science fair. My dedication to excellence—on the field and in the classroom—had become my new rhythm. Life moved fast, and the lake . . . well, it faded into the background like a childhood dream you don't mean to forget.

At the time, the lake felt like an old friend. But even then, there was something I couldn't quite name—an undercurrent, a stillness that wasn't peace but pause. It was as if the water was waiting for me to notice something, but I wasn't ready to see it. So I let it be.

Like Jackie Paper fading from Puff's world, I stopped returning. The lake, once alive with laughter and stones skipping like echoes of a heartbeat, had gone silent. Its fearless roar was gone—or so I thought.

"There was one gray night it happened; Jackie Paper came no more."

And so that mighty dragon slept and ceased his fearless roar. But nothing truly wild ever sleeps forever.

12

KEEP YOUR EYES ON THE WATER

As I delved into science, I found it comforting, clear, and structured, much like the projects in the magazines I devoured. In a way, it mirrored my life—a simple, neat, and predictable experiment. But even in the methodical world of chemistry, physics, and formulas, the lake kept calling, reminding me that some things couldn't be understood with equations alone. But I was preoccupied, on a different bandwidth and not getting the message.

I was drawn to science because it offered a logical, structured method for exploring answers to questions about how the world worked. The scientific method helped me sort out what was real and what wasn't.

However, I did not start out interested in science, as I was actively involved in too many sports. I did not have time to solve problems. I was too busy burying them. Playing sports was a great place to bury them and a diversion from problems.

By the time I reached middle school, I had discovered all the major American sports, starting with baseball. We played that throughout the summer. Then basketball and football were added to my calendar. Football had a short season since by October it usually was cold and blustery. By November, we'd have snow that wouldn't melt until April. The short fall and the long, dark, and frigid winter made basketball a popular sport. Due to my competitive spirit and persistence, I developed a mean jump shot and became the team's shooting guard and one of the top scorers.

By high school, however, my interest had shifted toward academics, particularly the hard sciences. The shift occurred gradually, yet at the conclusion of my sophomore year, my enthusiasm for science projects had surpassed my interest in sports. I exchanged my athletic gear for a lab coat, reinventing myself from a star athlete into a studious nerd.

Once I left competitive sports, I soon found myself serving as president of both the school science club and the school's National Honor Society. Based on my experience, which has evidence to support it, neither of these achievements led to many prom dates or romantic opportunities.

While a white lab coat doesn't exactly scream "heartthrob" the way a letterman jacket does, the dual president roles were not able to compensate for this. Prom dates and romantic opportunities were still as rare as the fans who came to cheer me on at the school science fairs. There I consistently achieved top results. In each of my four years of high school, my project advanced to the district level, and on one occasion, it progressed to the state science fair. Tangible rewards, such as trophies, fame, or recognition, were limited. Notably absent also were throngs of cheering fans. That didn't matter to me. My motivation stemmed from an intrinsic drive, a sincere passion, and a purpose that I did not fully understand at the time, but a letterman's jacket sure would have been nice.

Just as college scouts seek out promising athletes at sports competitions, there are individuals, especially at the state level, who actively seek out intellectual talent at science fairs. These recruiters represent reputable foundations of higher learning, searching for deserving candidates to help their institutions advance in the fields of science. I learned that including these activities on either a college application or a scholarship application can be a game-changer and significantly boost a resume. But I didn't need help with my résumé. I needed help with getting a date. It turns out, it wasn't my humble immigrant roots that scared off prom dates. It was the lab coat all along.

By the time I reached high school, the descriptor "poor immigrant" no longer fit me. Having made a courageous and challenging decision at the age of six, I had become a well-integrated, naturalized citizen of the United States, a true American who held a deep affection for his new homeland. If the NCAA had such a category, I would have been selected as an all-American American. But I suspect there would be many naturalized citizens in that space.

Much of the emotional baggage I carried from my past had been released and processed at the beach bootcamp. Under the watchful presence of the majestic Lake Superior, much like the relationship between Puff the Magic Dragon, and Little Jackie Paper, I had grown up and matured.

Despite my change of focus in school, sports weren't entirely out of the picture. It isn't easy to give up on the adrenaline rush and good energy levels that sports provide. It was not uncommon to see me in the street throwing footballs with my friend Dan, who, like me, had a good arm. We thoroughly enjoyed stretching our limits by tossing the ball over each other's heads, challenging each other to run under it and make impressive catches. We made this game our pastime.

We both would make catches that warranted coverage on the evening highlight reels. The spectacular catches were euphoric when they were met with success. When we didn't make a catch, well, sometimes more than our pride got hurt, like when I sprained my ankle while chasing one of Dan's long throws. I understood about the agony of defeat, as that aptly described my ankle's condition.

After painfully hobbling home, I went down to my room and sat on my bed, wondering what effect this would have on me. I certainly would miss throwing and catching the football, not to mention any other physical activity.

While mulling this over, I picked up my guitar and started playing a song with a lot of minor chords, which mirrored the way I was feeling. I was further discouraged when I dropped my pick on the floor and was unable to locate it. I got on the floor, reached under my bed, and found it. But during the search, my hand also encountered something that resembled a box.

Upon retrieving it, I found myself curious about its contents. Opening it, the first item that caught my attention was my deer hide–beaded headband, one of many creations from my "Indian" era when I was in grade school. Eager to rediscover this collection of childhood treasures, I promptly placed the headband on my head and continued to explore the rest of the box's contents. There were seagull feathers, which I had been gathering for a headdress I planned to make. There was a peace pipe and, in a deer hide leather sheath, the wooden knife I had carved. But it was when I took out the next item that I stopped in disbelief.

Just the other day, while I had been engaged in my morning Bible reading, I had come across the story of David and Goliath again. While reading it, my mind traveled back several years to the boy standing on his special beach. In his hand, he held a sling. In his pocket were five smooth stones; and a few extras. In front of him was his Goliath, a giant rock island far from throwing distance. He made it his challenge to hit that cliff-sided island with a stone launched from a sling, just like his hero David had when he killed his threatening giant.

That warm, vivid scene faded as quickly as it came, as I entertained thoughts that made me wonder how I would fare doing that exercise today. Obviously, I would do better now, but just how much better, intrigued me. That raised a more puzzling question: *What did I do with that sling?*

No sooner had I finished the thought when, underneath a tomahawk that I made with a real stone, there it was: the deer hide sling. The urge to do that same feat not only became irresistible, but now with the sling in hand, it was possible. It was no longer a question of if but when. And the answer that resonated was soon.

A few days later, with my ankle feeling a little better and the cooler fall weather broadcasting that winter was on its way, I got on the American Flyer with the sling holstered in my back pocket. As I pedaled east toward the lake, thoughts danced in my head like the wind-blown leaves swirling around my bike.

Wonder how far I can launch a stone now? It's been years since I have been to this special place. I wonder what it will be like. I was curious to see what Jackie Paper's return to the lake would be like. *Will the lake provide some autumn mist to frolic in like in the song?*

Realizing that this could evolve into a bigger deal than I thought, I pedaled faster. Arriving at the shore, I laid my bike on the rocks as I caught my breath and did a quick scan. Yup, nothing had changed in the three years since I last visited.

The smile of bright sun greeted me, but the threatening dark clouds racing in told me this was about to change. These dark, billowing clouds were something that I had not seen here before. Unlike the peaceful, easy feeling that I felt there previously, the current aura was unsettling, even fearful. *Is something wrong? Did I do something wrong? Where is this guilt coming from? This is home! I'm back! Jackie Paper has returned!*

But I wasn't here to celebrate a reunion. Judging from the look of the sky, there was no time for exercises in paranoia either. I had come to test myself on a new challenge, and my target, the rocky island, was disappearing in the fog like a shipwrecked dream right in front of me. It was the clock telling me that I didn't have much time.

Just as I pulled my sling from my back pocket, a gust of freezing wind came up, sending shivers down my spine, letting me know that "not much time" was now considered a generous prediction.

Despite my tender ankle, I needed to run, collect a few suitable stones, and attempt to launch them toward that island. The sun, now behind dark clouds, had been replaced by a strong wind coming off the lake. Standing near the water's edge, I could feel the wind intensifying. As the waves grew larger, I found myself retreating inland.

Realizing there was no chance to twirl my sling against the gusting wind, I reluctantly had to abort my mission and try on another day. The water's edge—where I was standing now—had moved twenty feet inland. And it was still coming. From my studies of Mishipizheu, one thing I learned was to keep my eyes on the water. Before I hurriedly removed myself from what was now becoming a dangerous situation, I studied the water. Under the challenging circumstances, I observed at least two aspects that caused me much concern. The first observation was quite evident. The three- to four-foot-high waves had me scrambling farther inland. It would have been much safer to observe the size of these waves from the edge of the woods, where I quickly retreated.

I remained there for several minutes as I watched the waves grow bigger, reaching four to five feet, covering the entire beach to the edge of the woods. I would have washed out to sea had I been standing on that beach one minute longer.

Why is the lake so angry? Is this Puff, roaring in fury? Is it because I had abandoned him like Jackie Paper did?

These thoughts raced through my head as I mounted my bike for the cold ride home. The freezing wind and the fact that I wasn't even given a chance to launch a rock at the island made the ride home miserable.

It was the second observation, however, that was so unsettling that I needed time to consider it before I could even discuss it. Naturally, this made the ride home as dreary as the stormy weather. My mind was preoccupied with troubling questions and thoughts all the way home. But one question kept echoing louder than the storm that chased me home: Why was the lake so angry?

Deep down, what scared me most was that I probably knew the answer.

13

WHAT ARE WE DRINKING

The brisk tailwind helped me pedal faster on the stormy ride home. This generated some warmth, which was welcome. Upon entering the house, the images of large waves coming at me stirred up long-forgotten memories of giant waves on the Atlantic Ocean. The pictures of increasingly larger waves could not be unseen any more than the questions each wave brought. The distress and agitation this caused had a dismaying effect on me, making me realize I was still in the midst of the storm.

It had been years since I had visited the beach that served as my training center, boot camp, mental health treatment center, and refuge from life's storms. Until now!

I wondered if I had been on the right beach. The impressive rock island, resembling a colossal Post Office, where I hoped to send a small package via air mail, assured me that I had the correct address. But everything else was unfamiliar, setting an ominous tone for some serious questions.

Was it just a mere coincidence that my return was accompanied by a dangerous situation unlike anything I had previously encountered there? Might this have been a message that the mighty dragon was conveying with his trademark fearless roar? If so, it was loud; I was left shaken.

When I retired for the night, I was kept awake, agitated by enormous waves washing over me. Finally, my eyes closed, and I fell into a restful sleep.

Suddenly, out of nowhere, a terrifying, colossal wave appeared. This immense wall of water moving toward me loomed ominously, threatening to crush me. From the heart of the wave, a sleek, black panther emerged, its piercing eyes gleaming with fury. The wave curled unnaturally, like it had a will. Then from the crest, it leapt—gleaming black fur, silent roar, those eyes. I woke up already running.

I was unable to process the fear of what I had just experienced, as a different kind of adrenaline had taken over when I realized I had overslept. *What did that mean?* was all I could think about as I ran to school as best I could on my sore ankle.

As I was making my way down the hall towards my civics class, I caught sight of Dan, who noticed me and came over to see how I was doing.

"How's the ankle?" Dan asked, enthusiastically. "Ready to chase down some long bombs?"

"Nah. It's not as painful," I replied, "but not strong enough for our aerial shows."

"So, how long do you think you need?"

"Couple of weeks. But right now, I'm dealing with some other things."

"What's going on?" Dan asked leaning in.

"Ahh, you might say my life's been a little stormy."

"Girls?"

"No! I don't have time right now," I said. "But if you're free tomorrow after school, let's go down to the Beaver, and I'll tell you about it."

"Kind of late for the smelt run, but I have nothing planned. Let's do it!"

"I'll see you then!"

Two nearby rivers emptied into Lake Superior, one on each side of Silver Bay. The Beaver River, two miles to the south, was more popular because there was a sunny beach nestled in a cove adjacent to its mouth, which was the reason I wanted to go there. The river and the beach were a popular spot for us high school students to gather, especially during the annual smelt spawning runs in April, when the river was teeming with so many small fish they could be caught by hand. But Dan and I weren't going there for fish. I had something else in mind. I was still preoccupied with the second thing I saw during the storm. I was curious to know if I would see it at this other beach, so we started on the three-mile bike ride.

During our ride on the backroads to the Beaver, I told Dan about the menacing storm I had encountered a few days ago, along with the frightening wave that brought out a scary panther in my nightmare. I withheld what I saw in the water, waiting to see what we would find when we arrived. After parking our bikes between pine trees at the edge of the shore, we walked across the beach. At the water's edge, gentle waves could not conceal what I anticipated finding. "Look at that! There it is." I exclaimed in unrestrained excitement just as the sun went behind a small cloud.

"Look at what?" Dan asked. "Haven't you ever seen water before?"

"No! Look! Don't you see that the water isn't clear?"

"Hey, I don't know how many times we've gotten a drink right out of the lake here, like dogs. Are you trying to scare me, tell me there's something wrong with the water?"

Just then, I noticed a can on the beach near us. After retrieving it, I took out my knife and cut off the top. Wading out a short way, I reached down and scooped up some water and looked at it closely. "Here, would you drink this?" I asked, holding out the can.

"Well, it is a little murky and not really clear. I don't know."

I was satisfied. The observations I made here corroborated my previous ones, and I did not feel any fear about being carried out to sea this time. Having Dan there validated that I wasn't seeing things or going crazy. He would come in handy.

On the ride home, I couldn't stop thinking about the storm and the terrifying nightmare that followed it. What was the significance of one right after the other? And Puff's dramatic roar, expressed in the angry storm that greeted me after years of absence, was that because of me, or for me? Was there a message? Was the terrifying panther repeating it? In my previous experiences with both, I had seen neither that angry. Was this a summons?

Although I had informed Dan of my storm story, he was still disappointed that it wasn't about girls. So, I began thinking up a plan that included him. We stopped by the school, and seeing that Mr. B's car was still there, I went in to set up a meeting for the three of us for the next day after school.

Mr. B was the quintessential science teacher. He was tall and lanky and wore dark-rimmed glasses and was never seen without a white lab coat. He served as the advisor for the school's science club, of which I had the honor of being president.

The following day in chemistry, Mr. B started the class holding an apple over his head. He let it go and caught it before it smashed on the floor. "Millions of people had seen apples fall. But only one person asked the right question. And what an easy question that was: Why? That person, Isaac Newton, was a scientist." Setting the apple on his desk, he continued, "A scientist is not a person who has all the right answers, but one who asks the right questions. When you work on your experiments today, keep that in mind. Someone made every great advance in science with an inquisitive imagination and the audacity to ask the right questions."

Before he even finished, I thought, *Wow! Did he ever set us up for our meeting.*

After the last class, Dan and I went up to see Mr. B in his classroom. When we walked into the room, he was waiting for us, sitting at his desk, still in his lab coat. Dan and I sat across from him, looking serious and buzzing with adrenaline. A late afternoon light spilled across the desks as the meeting started. Mr. B removed his glasses and studied my face. "Well, gentlemen," he started. "You look like you've just returned from a lab experiment gone sideways. What's on your mind?"

"It's about the lake," I replied with a sigh. "I've been out to two different beaches in the past week. Both times the water was, well, off. Murky. Not like it used to be."

"Yeah," Dan said, nodding his head. "I saw it too. We were at the Beaver. Water's always been clean enough to drink there. This time, it wasn't."

"And it wasn't just what we saw," I added. "It was what I felt. The storm that hit a few days ago was the craziest one I've seen. The lake felt . . . angry. Like something's not right. It felt personal."

Mr. B, frowning, replied, "Angry? That's poetic. But you're saying this murkiness—was it like sediment? Or discoloration?"

"From what I saw at the Beaver, both," I replied. "But I'm not sure yet. I haven't tested it. That's why we're here. We have a plan. But first, we need your help setting the stage."

Mr. B leaned back, intrigued. "All right, I'm listening."

"Tomorrow in chemistry, I'd like you to ask the class how many of them have been to the lake lately and noticed the water looking murky or discolored. Then ask them if it ever occurred to them to question whether it's safe to drink straight from the lake like we've always done."

Mr. B nodded slowly. "And this is to determine whether others have noticed or are concerned?"

"Exactly! If people start asking the right questions, then we've got consensus. Our science club can get water samples and run tests to figure out if there's contamination or not."

"We just want to know what we're drinking," Dan said quietly.

Mr. B, smiled for a moment and then said, "Not a bad plan. You know, asking the right questions is how Newton started. But it's also how revolutions start."

"Then I guess tomorrow's lesson might start one," I quipped.

As Dan and I left, we saw Mr. B reaching for his chalk. We paused as he wrote "ASK WHY" on the board, underlining it twice.

14

TAKING A STAND

The following day, Mr. B started his lecture by saying, "As we delve further into the scientific method and the significance of inquiry, I would like to begin our class with a survey." Both Dan and I leaned forward in our seats. As if reading from a script, Mr. B inquired, "How many of you have recently visited the lake and observed that the water looked murky or discolored?" Dan and I, as if propelled by springs, simultaneously raised our hands and surveyed the room. We observed four other hands that were raised.

Mr. B kept going. "Did you ever wonder if it's safe to drink straight from the lake?" he asked, sternly. With that he gave us a nod and then continued with his lecture. He explained that observation and posing the right questions are fundamental to science, but that answers must be pursued through experimentation and the gathering of facts.

Mr. B, ever the science evangelist, praised student-led inquiry, the holy grail of learning, as he called it. That segued into an explanation of my plan to collect water samples and conduct tests on them. Half of the class expressed an interest in this and offered their assistance, stemming from suspected reservations some may have had during their last visit to the lake.

Mr. B was cautiously pleased and pulled me aside as I was leaving the room. "What if—"

"We found something wrong with the water," I finished his sentence for him. "Then science has done its job and provided us with knowledge. But if that knowledge doesn't lead to action, science has failed us."

"There's that revolutionary talk again," he replied as I hurried to my next class.

The project got started in late September 1968, my senior year. We collected water samples from six designated locations within the Reserve plant's perimeter. We recorded the pH levels at each site, and labeled the bottles and refrigerated them until we were ready to run a series of tests on them.

Given concerns about murkiness, one such test focused on quantifying the amount of suspended solids.

First, we measured a beaker's tare weight (or weight when it was empty). Then we poured some of the sample water into the beaker and brought it to a boil. After the water was boiled off, we reweighed the beaker. We ran several other tests to measure the turbidity (or cloudiness) of the water, including ones that utilized our lab microscope.

Two of the six water samples came from the Beaver and Baptism Rivers, which served as our natural control samples.

When the analysis phase was finally completed, I took the lab book home, eager to see if the results confirmed my suspicions. I was up late, writing, being careful to report the results honestly and factually. The next morning, I took the report to Mr. B, who read it as I waited for his response. Once he finished reading the report, he put it down and was quiet for a long time. He finally spoke softly. "You're not wrong. But it is a little puzzling. What are you planning to do with this report?"

My hands clenched the edge of my chair. I wasn't sure if I was defending a report or lighting a fuse. Calmly, I replied, "Beyond giving it to you, I haven't decided. Several concerned students contributed to the study. I feel obligated to share the findings with them as a reward for their commitment."

Picking up my report, Mr. B responded, "Yeah, regarding the students' concerns, I read your entire report, and none of your findings addressed them nor answered their questions."

Like a flood, an uncontrollable inner voice emerged, speaking not for me but for something else. "You have taught us it's important to ask questions. The students weren't asking the right ones. They saw the murky, discolored water. Out of fear, the only question on their mind was, Is it safe to drink?" Catching my breath, I continued, "If we were trying to find out if it's safe to drink, then our study failed because we didn't have the right tools. But we weren't doing that."

With a puzzled look, Mr. B responded, "Let me try to understand what you're saying. This study was not conducted to determine whether the lake water was safe to drink straight from the lake. You did it to . . ."

When his voice trailed off, I felt like I was being backed into a corner. Trying to show respect and acknowledge his role as my teacher, I spoke passionately. "When I became aware of water abnormalities at two different lake locations, my first thought wasn't Is this safe to drink?" As I paused, I felt an adrenaline surge as words came rushing out. "No! My first reaction wasn't fear. It was Why. The same, simple question that the guy who couldn't hold on to apples asked."

Mr. B cracked a faint smile, acknowledging I had made a good point. Satisfied, I continued, "As we know, the apple guy's Why led to a great discovery. That is NOT the case here. Me, you, and everyone in this town know EXACTLY *WHY* the water is murky and—"

"We're getting into deep waters here," Mr. B interrupted. "Let's change that to we *think* we know why." I acknowledged his effort to smooth out what was turning into a tempest. He continued, "Since you *think* you know why the water was murky, your interest was in what you *suspected* to be the source." Mr. B furrowed his brow and continued, "So, what you're saying is this wasn't about safety. It was about finding the source."

Realizing he was going too far, he quickly shut it down. "I believe it will be necessary to speak with our principal about this," he said. "Please be assured that you are not facing any repercussions from either me or the school." After adjusting his glasses, he continued, "Although I have problems with the nature of your study, I can't fault either your work or your conviction. The principal must be informed before hearing it from someone else. Would you be amenable to a meeting between the three of us before you discuss your findings with peers?"

"Sure, let me know when you want me to be there."

Thankfully, that ended the meeting as I had run out of room in the corner.

15

PRINCIPAL'S OFFICE SUMMIT

The following morning, having been informed of the meeting, I found myself walking to the principal's office, unsure what Mr. Lee might ask—and how I'd respond. It felt like I was being thrown into a lion's den.

When I arrived, Mr. Lee sat behind his desk, and Mr. B occupied the chair adjacent to him. After a quick exchange of pleasantries, Mr. Lee got right to it. "George," he said, "I've heard a lot about you. You're one of the top students in your class. Your role as science club president and the projects you've led are exemplary. But this latest one raises concerns."

That was the setup. Fear gripped me as I braced for what came next.

"After reviewing your report, I have some questions."

It was like standing on that beach again, bracing for two-foot waves—but this time I was paralyzed. My heart pounded as he started firing them off.

"First of all, have you shared this with anyone?" Mr. Lee asked.

"No, sir. Only with Mr. B."

"Good. And what was your purpose for doing this study?" His eyes narrowed. He wasn't just asking; he was measuring. I glanced at Mr. B, who leaned forward slightly. *Looks like Lee's wasting no time. I won't either,* I thought.

"Yes, there seems to be a misunderstanding about that," I replied in a calm tone. Locked in on Mr. Lee, I spoke my piece, a little shaky at first. "I believe we all recognize the importance of the big plant on the lake shore," I began. I cut right to the chase. Mr. Lee didn't summon me here for a science lesson—or a primer on lab protocols. Besides, I left my lab coat upstairs. From my perspective, we were here to talk about a pending storm— and a high-stakes moral crisis. And Mr. Lee wasn't here to challenge the data in my report. He couldn't. The facts spoke for themselves—and so did the water samples. His second question, my motives, was aimed at the real target.

The report didn't reveal anything new. Anyone with eyes and half a conscience could walk along the lake shore, *keep their eyes on the waters,* and see the truth. My report was a speeding ticket, nothing more. A notice that says pay attention; you're going too fast, and someone's going to get hurt. If they want to attack my report, I'll help them. I have my own issue with it; it's far too superficial. It's a speeding ticket issued after an accident. Sure, it's done, but it's too late. What's needed now is an assessment of the damage. A follow-up study needs to focus on what impact the plant has on the lake's ecosystem.

I wasn't holding back. I wasn't on trial. The future of the lake was. And I wasn't going to negotiate that away. My words poured out like a river with no dam to stop them. What did I have to lose?

As it turns out—a lot. But I had a role to play. One summoned by an angry black panther, rising out of a terrifying wave in my dream. I closed out my explanation by doubling down not once but twice. Looking at Mr. B, I calmly started with, "Many saw the problems with the lake water. But only one person dared to ask *why*—and issue the speeding ticket."

I looked again at Mr. B and saw a wide grin spreading across his face, his head rocking side to side. I knew what he was thinking: *I can't believe you used that line two days in a row—and this time in front of my boss.* I wasn't trying to be cheeky or disrespectful. I wanted Mr. Lee to see what kind of teacher Mr. B was—how his students listened and *applied* what he taught. But I doubt either of them caught that.

Winded, I handed the metaphorical gavel back to Mr. Lee. "I didn't mean to practice my valedictorian speech on you both." I remarked with a tongue-in-cheek tone, "I just wanted to provide some context. Do you have any other concerns or questions?"

Mr. Lee replied with a smirk, "I can't say it was a good speech, but not bad for a tale. Though your main character needs help with his costume. Instead of a police uniform, he should have worn knight's armor. Silver Bay isn't a fairy tale town, George. It's not some mythical, medieval village. It's a business town. A mining town. No castles on hills here. Just a big plant on a big lake. Showing up like a knight in shining armor, raising a sword? That's rich, and remarkably naive."

As he paused, I chewed on what he said. *So, he sees me as a naive knight with sword in his hand*, I thought. I liked the image, especially the part about the sword. Beats the visual of me with a radar gun and clipboard. I wondered if there was a deeper meaning in the sword, Siegfried's sword?

Nah. Better watch my backside. Lee's good at setups—and denials.

Mr. Lee continued, "You've lived here long enough to know how this town works. But since you like allegories, I'll give you one. There's a big mining plant run by one we will call the king. And then there are the residents, the serfs. Most of the serfs work for the king. He pays them well. Gives them an idyllic lifestyle. They're happy. He's a benevolent king. He built this shire for the serfs to live in. He put it on the map where twenty years ago there was just wilderness."

"Okay, I get that!" I cut in, unable to hold back. "I appreciate the king just as much as any other serf in the shire. Holy cow, this school he built for us young serfs is second to none! The problem I have is, well, he's kind of messy."

THE KING'S PROTOCOL

Before I could respond, Mr. Lee's face grew flushed, and he tightened his fists as he erupted: "Okay, George, here's something you need to understand. There is *one rule* in this shire: You keep your nose clean, and YOU DON'T ATTACK THE KING. That's the king's protocol. That's how this place is run. Follow it, and you live long and prosper. Break it, and you suffer the consequences."

I sighed. "Mr. Lee," I replied, "I understand it better than you think. And like waves gathering strength, I'm already feeling the backlash. There's a price. There's a cost. The serfs will turn on me. The king will roar—even turn into a dragon. That's what happens when the emperor walks around naked and someone dares to say it aloud."

I paused, letting the next words settle in.

"I didn't do this lightly," I continued. "I've been wrestling with the consequences since I began the study. Challenging decisions aren't new to me; they are in my DNA."

I glanced at Mr. B, who had been silent until now. He fidgeted, clearly wanting to speak. "George," he began softly, "I think you are one of the brightest students I have ever had. I have seen how you study in my classes and your work on your science fair projects. Given your position as the male valedictorian, it is highly likely that you will be the recipient of the Reserve Mining Company's annual scholarship, a full four-year ride. I hate seeing you not get it."

I nodded. "Thank you, Mr. B. That means a lot coming from you. Honestly, ever since I started high school, that scholarship's been on my radar screen. You know my background. As an immigrant, we're trained to spot shiny objects and work like mad to earn them. I've never felt privileged or entitled—just deserving. But

I'm afraid this time, that protocol will be broken. The company has awarded that scholarship to the top male and female students for the last twelve years. But that ship sailed when I chose to move forward—knowing exactly what it might cost."

Mr. Lee, practically coming unglued, responded, "George, then *why* did you do it? You don't come across as the crazy type."

Touché! Well played! Mr. B, did you notice that somebody else asks Why questions?

Before Mr. Lee spontaneously combusted, I replied. "I assure you, Mr. Lee, that I don't have a death wish. But if you really want to know, since you asked the Why question, I will . . ."

I couldn't finish the sentence before I was overtaken by something. I looked through the window where I could see Lake Superior less than a mile away. As I raised my head and closed my eyes, I took a deep breath and paused for a long time, savoring the peace and the spirit that had overtaken me. I knew what was coming.

THE CREATOR'S PROTOCOL

Glancing over at Mr. B, I met Mr. Lee's unwavering stare without flinching.

"Mr. Lee," I continued, "your explanation of the king's protocol, which governs life in the shire, was indeed enlightening and was taken to heart. However, I learned and adopted another protocol, even more crucial in human governance. I refer to it as the Creator's protocol. Let me explain, but don't worry, I'm not going to give you a sermon. In fact, regrettably, it is likely that you might never hear this in any sermon, nor would children hear it in their Sunday school classes, although they should.

"The foundation of this protocol is found in the initial three chapters of the Bible, which describe God's creation and a beautiful garden, more idyllic than a romanticized medieval village. It is there that the Creator placed a man and a woman. One of the few instructions the man was given by his Creator was to work and take care of God's creation. That is the Creator's protocol, and it overrides the king's protocols.

"I learned this not in church but from my studies of Native American Indians and by spending time on the shores of Lake Superior. We may be the settler serfs of Silver Bay, but don't kid yourself, we're not the first people here. There was a whole other race of people, some of whom are buried in the Indian burial grounds in Beaver Bay. These people, our predecessors, were the Chippewa or Ojibwe Indians. Their beliefs and values are foreign to us and even to orthodox Judeo-Christian beliefs. But I assure you, they align with the Creator's protocol, which is sacrosanct among them.

"Here is what I learned and adopted from their beliefs: The Chippewa believe their land is sacred. (You will never hear that word used in our shire.) They believe they belong to the land and not the other way around. They believe they are sojourners, and they work on their land and mine it to survive, but they don't abuse or harm it and leave a mess for the people who follow them."

I paused to let that sink in.

"Chippewa have honor, and their word means something. (That's why you don't see them in politics.) Last, but not least, and this is personal to me, the Chippewas believe in powerful spirits that protect their sacred lands. They revere and fear these spirits. One such spirit that I have come to know through time spent at the lake is Mishipizheu, the lake's guardian. He has two sides to him, a black panther, if you're a good person, and a dragon for the bad people who don't follow the Creator's protocol, who cause harm and abuse the lake."

I knew that last statement was lighting a fuse. I didn't realize how short it was because as soon as I finished, both Mr. Lee and Mr. B broke out in the biggest belly laugh. I couldn't determine whether it stemmed from fear or conviction.

When he finally stopped laughing, Mr. Lee said, "Thank you, George, for telling us we're bad people and warning us of the wrath to come, presumably in the form of a dragon. If that happens, I wonder if you could show up again, not in your policeman uniform, but as a knight with that great sword in your hand."

I told them where I stood by answering his Why question. I'm sure it didn't get through to him. But I didn't need the ridicule. He was in a position of authority after all. His fear was that the king's knights could appear at any time, demanding to know what was going on. Thankfully, Mr. B seemed to get it. He was slowly shaking his head. That told me he didn't support Mr. Lee's comment.

Get used to it. What's a little ridicule? I'm sure things will get worse, I told myself. *Glad that long meeting is over.*

The big question was how quickly and badly this was going to get. I did my job and stood my ground. I left the speeding ticket on Mr. Lee's desk. And the fire alarm, which I had pulled, was sounding.

16

COMMUNICATIONS IN THE SHIRE

With a big sigh of relief, I opened the door to leave Mr. Lee's office. I was greeted by a throng of students. *Why are they here?* I wondered. Then I got the picture.

Our shire was equipped with a "high-speed communication network" before the modern systems existed. I refer to it as the *serfnet,* which operated using the proprietary *teleserf* protocol. Technically, the teleserf protocol operated like a blockchain over the serfnet. It was a tech engineer's dream—unlimited bandwidth, scalability, and incident-free throughput.

The serfs, from which the protocol derived its name, used primitive hardware consisting of handheld devices hardwired to a wall mounted unit. They could be logged into uninterrupted communication sessions lasting hours, holding their overheated handhelds in their cramped hands. Because they were tethered to a wall unit, remote operation was not possible.

However, there was a complementary part of the serfnet that allowed remote operation. It used "Bluetooth" that functioned over the teleserf protocol. This enabled lightning-fast, wireless, remote communication. Unlike modern Bluetooth technology that requires pairing, the shire's version was voice-activated, session-dependent, and seamless. To connect to, or "Bluetooth," a peer, you simply talked to them. To end your session, you walked away and you were unpaired.

The shire's communication system was not only efficient but was virtually unbreakable. In twelve years, I had never seen a meltdown. Secretly, I was hoping for one now. It was these two components, serfs spreading the news on the tethered handhelds and serfs remotely connecting with other serfs that spread the news like an out-of-control wildfire through the shire. This explains how quickly the flash mob appeared outside Mr. Lee's office.

To understand this telecom system and how quickly news could be spread through the shire, it was necessary to delve into more technical details than I wanted to. That generally happens in discussions about telecom systems. I hate it too! But this is important to understand as it reveals why news could travel so quickly through the shire. I'm sure many small towns operate with similar systems. The entire mission and special ops plan that I was part of relied on this system. Cutting through the tech talk, here is a simplified breakdown of how the telecom system helped accomplish the mission:

Want to spread news? Tell a serf.

Want it to go viral? Tell a group of serfs and watch the protocol take over.

A feature of this serfnet was that it offered full anonymity and zero regulation, provided the king wasn't criticized. Zero may be a stretch. There was self-regulation. Here is how it worked:

Every serf, including me, using the serfnet, was groomed to follow the king's protocol. There was only one rule: don't say anything bad about the king. In this case, telling news that the king is making a mess in the lake would have earned me a crowd of serfs quicker than the one that showed up outside of Mr. Lee's office, only they'd have pitchforks. I'd also land on the king's "Praetorian Knights" watch list. But I'm sure I was already on that. With only a single rule, this programming was used to silence opposition to the king's authority, particularly if he was doing something wrong—a precursor to the modern political correctness movement.

To understand how I was part of a special ops PSYOP that was used to work around the king's protocol and carry out the mission, I will roll back and narrate a declassified black-and-white film.

There! In the first scene, I saw the murky, discolored water.

I remarked, "Do you see what is in water?"

Dan replied in *serftalk*: "See what? Naaah! It always looks like that! Come on, George, next you'll have me believing conspiracy theories."

The tape rolls showing me, without proper resources, finding a can on the beach. Quickly turning it into a makeshift cup, I scoop up some water and hand it to Dan, saying, "Look at this! Would you drink it?" The Decoy. I create a stake or a personal concern, and Dan "feels" the problem in the water that he doesn't "see."

Dan replies, "I don't know, it doesn't look good. What do you think?"

"I agree!" Ally created.

We move on to the next two scenes, with the teacher and the class. The strategy was the same: personalize the water problem and make it a safety concern. Let them feel the problem. Many students have drunk water directly from the lake. Like picking low-hanging fruit, it was easy to sell a study that focused on lake water safety. Though unseen, it could be felt. More allies were created, including a teacher.

The students were the low-hanging fruit. Easy.

Three things you never saw in Silver Bay: a cell phone, a water bottle, and a portable water filter. Whether on foot or on bike, if you were thirsty and close to the lake, you went down and got a drink of cold water the same way dogs did.

Halfway through the plan, the alarm was already sounding. The volume just wasn't turned up yet. This explained the waiting crowd. But not *who* was in it. Some were allies from the water study group. Check. But most were unaffiliates, including jocks I used to compete against. They were easy to spot as they wore letterman jackets.

But what were they doing here? That told me the storm and waves were building momentum. Traffic on the serfnet was ramping up. And the entire shire was a hotspot.

THE SPECIAL OPS COA DECLASSIFIED.

Let me decode this special ops plan Course Of Action.

It started with the panther's angry roar. That wasn't just a dream. It was a download! A mission brief. A call-up order from something older than the king.

I'd been asleep. Worse—I'd been blind.

The lake, an old friend, was dying.

The cause? A messy, powerful king who no one dared confront.

And somehow, I got picked to be David.

My weapon wasn't just a sling. It was a plan. Protocol be damned.

The mission's declassified Course Of Action had a simple five-step plan:

1. Observe the sickness.
2. Recruit the skeptic.
3. Let him feel the truth.
4. Turn emotion into alliance.
5. Expand the alliance with an investigation to awaken the town by flooding the serfnet with a PSYOP gone viral.

It involved misdirection. Truth was encoded in packets of a politically correct narrative that was fueled by suspicion and fear.

A shrewd Mr. Lee was correct in challenging my motives. But like the speeding ticket, he was too late.

The crowd showed me that. I was happy they left their pitchforks at home.

And speaking of pitchforks, there are two unanswered questions that could potentially arise: First, how was the town actually awakened to the problem that the plant was polluting Lake Superior? Second, how was I treated?

The simple answer is that fear can improve your vision. But not always.

It is true that people's fears were initially focused on personal safety, specifically whether the lake water was safe. That was the only way they would look at it. When no answers were offered, fear gave way to anger.

People got angry that no one was providing answers. Lunchroom table discussions were seasoned with frustration masquerading in comments like, "What'd you hear" and "me neither!"

In locker rooms, you might hear: "Hey, have you heard anything about the water?"

Students at home holding a glass of water from the kitchen faucet asked their parents, "Do you think this is safe?"

Those questions were becoming more common. They didn't violate the king's protocol. The king had heard them before. The official answer was always:

> Do not be concerned about the appearance
> of the lake water. We have conducted studies
> to address those concerns. Our findings
> indicate that the tailings we process are
> transported far into the lake and deposited

into a very deep trough, where they settle to the bottom.

Sure, they do. The only thing more unbelievable than their official statement is how long people believed it despite the evidence right in front of them that told a different story. Fueled by strong emotions, things were changing. Eyes suddenly saw something different. Regal orthodoxy was challenged. People saw the problem. It wasn't about water being safe to drink. It was about the lake being safe from the king. The town was awakened. Mission accomplished.

NIGHT OF THE DREAM

That night I went to sleep with mixed feelings. Thoughts were swirling through my mind like leaves caught in a whirlwind, thoughts of what I had done and what had been done to me. The thoughts morphed into scenes that flashed by like an editorialized newsreel of my life.

The agonizing scene of a young boy, bitterly weeping in his grandmother's living room, painfully crying, "I don't know, I don't know!"

A scene of a timid, frightened young boy hiding himself behind his teacher, afraid.

I observed a lovely lakeshore scene with water glistening under the sunlight. In stark contrast, I saw an adolescent who was clearly distressed walking along the beach.

My grandmother, Ahne, appeared as the guardian of the first six years of my life. She was not only the guardian but the architect, creating a life so idyllic I could have been mistaken for a fairy tale character surrounded by

> castles
>> dragons
>>> panthers and
>>>> knights

Slow down! My mind was racing now.

There he was—Siegfried, the Norse legend and my childhood hero and role model of bravery. I saw technicolor images of Siegfried overcoming a dragon in a battle that lasted days. Its blood covered his whole body and became Siegfried's guardian, one that was as close to him as his own skin.

I saw the falling linden leaf, which prevented blood from covering a spot on his back, creating a vulnerability. Sadly, an enemy exploited that with a spear. I wondered what happened to his magnificent sword.

The images kept returning to the lakeshore scene with a solitary, depressed figure. That was me! I never encountered another person there, yet I felt seen. More importantly, I was felt by an unseen presence. How did I know? I didn't. It was a presence. None of my five senses can observe a presence.

The stream of visuals and narrations was enlightening. But I wished I could get to sleep.

One thought kept coming up. How did I know that my presence had been felt when I was walking on that beach? It was a comforting thought, but where were the receipts?

Thankfully, the answer, like a sudden lake storm, came quickly. During those dark times, I was asking tough questions:

Why am I here?

What is my purpose?

Why did I come here?

Like waves lapping at my feet, I asked these questions repeatedly while pacing along the shore. Nobody was there to hear me. But I was talking to someone. Not with my voice but with my heart. A heart cries. It shows passion. It must be felt.

But not getting answers to my essential questions challenged me like reps with heavy weights in the gym.

I was building my patience muscles. Patience built my character. My character made me strong enough to stand and not buckle under pressure.

My first battle was with myself.

High stakes.

Keep believing.

Keep trusting.

Don't give up.

Don't back down.

You are in the gym.

Keep doing the reps.

What do you have to lose?

This sounded like a revisit of my basic training. I was being shown what changed me and how far I had come.

Then, like an enveloping fog that changes the mood, an image of Mr. Lee sitting at his desk appeared. It was his wily imagination that painted me as the knight in shining armor with a sword in his hand. It was blatant mockery. Full stop!

But I accepted it as a fantastic compliment on many levels!

- He made me into a hero in a fairy tale world—his! That was rich!
- He transformed an American mining town into a medieval shire. Thank you.

- And last, but not least, he cast himself as the black knight in this story. Well done, sir!

More than I knew, he tried to take me out. With his scrawny falchion, he tried to find my weakness. Ahne warned me about people like this. But I wouldn't show him my backside. I withstood him—boldly and bravely—and walked out to an awaiting crowd. Regrettably, they weren't cheering. They were curious, anxious, and fearful.

But he wasn't defeated; he just went away to scheme up a dastardly plan against me.

∽

My graduating class was the twelfth in the school's history. In the preceding eleven classes, the top-performing male and female students were chosen as co-valedictorians. In each of those years, the Reserve scholarship was automatically granted to those class valedictorians.

In my graduating year, the school decided to change the valedictorian honor. It established two categories of scholars: Honors and Highest Honors, with several students in each group meeting the newly adopted criteria. When I saw that, I was heartbroken, and I realized that they had just cheated me out of an honor that I had worked hard for four years to earn.

This was not just wrong! It was suspicious. Mr. Lee was behind it to cover for the king. If the plan were to deny me the scholarship given to the top eleven previous male valedictorians, their actions would be obvious. The entire town would see that as wrong. But if I were one of the five Highest Honors candidates and someone else was awarded it, nobody would notice.

I'm sure Mr. Lee and his school "referees" changed the rules while the game was still being played, so it wouldn't look so bad when the king kept me from scoring.

Mr. Lee may have stolen my honor, but he couldn't steal my valor.

FOLLOW THE LIGHT

Exhausted and disheartened, I finally drifted off into a deep sleep—pulled not into rest but summoned. The kind that doesn't ask for your presence; it claims it.

Suddenly, I was in a rushing river! But it's not water. I'm caught up in a current of puffy clouds, racing past at dizzying speed. I accelerated breathlessly through shifting skies, unable to respond. Something stirs deep inside me as I'm carried forward, flying without wings, without a plane, just pure motion through clouds that shift from green to blue to crimson. Then everything stops.

The colors vanish.

Blackness swallows all.

A foreboding uneasiness settles in thick and unyieldingly. Anxiety pulses through my veins as time seems to dissolve into an endless void. Far ahead a pinpoint of light appears. It grows, widening into a piercing ray that cuts through the darkness. Shapes emerge—a black throne, cold and immovable, carved with ancient markings as if from volcanic stone. Heavy mist curls around it, chilling me to the bone. Beside the throne sits a black panther, motionless and regal. His amber eyes lock onto mine—not threatening but unwavering.

Between his teeth rests a scabbard, etched with symbols from another age.

From the mist, a towering figure begins to take form—his presence cloaked in fog, his eyes burning like fire. He studies me with a stern, unblinking gaze, as if reading the deepest corners of my soul.

He turns to the panther. Slowly, he reaches out and draws a sword from the scabbard. The steel gleams as he holds it in his right hand. Time halts. I cannot move.

Again, he turns to the panther. The great cat nods once. Then the figure shifts the sword toward me. He pauses. The moment stretches into eternity.

Lowering his head, he raises the blade high above him. Light explodes from the steel, so brilliant it sears my eyes, forcing me to turn away. When I look again, he nods and lowers the weapon—not to strike but as an offering. I'm unable to move—whether frozen in awe or by fear, I cannot tell.

As the sword nears, a voice echoes from nowhere and everywhere at once: "Follow the light."

I jolt awake—heart pounding, breath ragged. My mind struggles to make sense of the dream's meaning.

By morning, the images have faded, but the words remain, circling in my thoughts like something half-remembered—waiting.

THE SUPERIOR GUARDIAN

As the first rays of sunlight crept through the curtains, my eyes snapped open, and I was immediately conscious. Trying to make sense of the dream I wondered, *Did I die and just watch a review of my life in heaven?* The last throne scene with the ancient being left me breathless and utterly astounded.

What was that all about? I didn't know, but I felt renewed and inspired.

It was a new day and a new chapter in my life. Indeed, the times were a-changin', as a famous folk singer, who grew up sixty miles from me, sang. (No, we never met.)

I had graduated and would be off to college in the fall. One thing I was looking forward to was anonymity. I had unintentionally made myself known, not as a celebrity rock star but as a troublemaker. I aspired to be neither. I was still as uncomfortable with the spotlight as I was in that frozen kindergarten scene.

One impressive thing the restless night of watching scenes from my life showed me was how far I had come. From the hysterical boy in Ahne's *Stube,* resisting extraction from an idyllic life, to the terrified boy in the hold of a battleship, who arrived like a destitute alien in another world. I found comfort and purpose in solitude where an unspoken voice had been an unwavering reminder that I was not alone.

I had found purpose. More importantly, I had found myself. And I was proud of who I had become. I wasn't the brave knight of my childhood dreams. But I learned to wield his sword as my biggest adversary found out.

I wasn't the Pied Piper, but I was transformational. I transformed a mining town into a medieval village, much like the one I came from. In the process, I woke up five thousand pairs of eyes, and they saw what they had refused to see.

I was the harbinger, warning of drastic changes to come. And they did come not long after I left for college. I had lit the fuse.

Redemption was coming. Action would be taken to keep a critical wound from spreading. Healing would follow. The Creator's protocol would be honored, and Mishipizheu and the Ojibwe would be happy.

As for the town, painful changes came that left people shocked, bewildered, and lost. There was a cost. I say that neither dispassionately nor out of spiteful vengeance. I paid a price, and it cost me.

My heart went out to my friends and everyone I knew in school. Everyone had fathers who worked at the plant, including me. All the fathers feared what might happen. All their children were concerned. I was one of them.

Lest this story turn into a dirge, I will focus on my father. While he was not an enthusiastic supporter of what I was doing, neither was he a panicked parent who feared losing his job because of it. How interesting.

From time to time, he would ask me how things were going and what I was doing. It seemed obligatory, especially when he told me how his peers at work were treating him. He was being harassed, told to get his crazy son to stop what he was doing before they all lose their jobs. And worse.

Like me, he was shunned, ostracized, and attacked. He sat alone during his breaks. People talked about him behind his back. But he used none of that to manipulate me into stopping my work. He never complained about becoming a victim or to vent his fears. That would have violated our unspoken family motto: We are not victims.

Although not openly supportive of what I was doing, the situation was different privately. My water study may have had an influence, but it's doubtful he was a secret convert. He had his own epiphany and plan. That explains why he wasn't defensive when, out of concern, I told him, "Papa, you need to look for a new job." That would not help most teenagers get the car next weekend. (Back in those days, no teenager owned their own car. If you had a weekend date, you had to behave and comply with your father's protocol and ask to borrow the car. Compliance required meeting standards most teens today would not be able to meet.)

People were genuinely afraid of losing their job. More so because the Plant treated its workers so royally. In addition to good pay and benefits, the company, under a union contract, offered every employee a thirteen-week vacation every five years.

My father, during his second thirteen-week vacation, was working in a large brewery in Colorado that summer. When he came home at the halfway point, he had a major surprise.

"We are moving to Colorado!" he announced.

"What? Did you quit your job at Reserve?" I asked.

"No, we are moving out there first. Before my vacation is up, I will give them my two-week notice."

"Paaapa! That's double-dipping. Is that okay to do?"

It turns out that it was not just okay, it was great! I was incredibly happy for him and us.

What do you know? All along, he had been quietly building an ark. Well played! He was not going to be a victim in the coming apocalypse. He was shutting the door and heading for higher ground, Colorado!

I was elated! I had dreamed of attending college in Colorado for years. Out-of-state tuition and the lack of a scholarship prevented me from pursuing it. Being a resident would at least alleviate the tuition problem. Dad must have had me in mind when he created a spare room in his ark.

We were headed for Colorado! But now I would have to learn about cowboys.

Still, before I could move forward, I needed to visit an old friend. I had a score to settle.

For what would be the final time, I rode down to the lake, my sling tucked securely in my back pocket. That rocky island believed it had gotten rid of me, like a pesky seagull.

How inconsiderate that the last time I was there it conjured up a storm with the largest waves I had ever witnessed on the lake. When I got to the lake, it was overcast. Really? Are we going to try that again? It didn't scare me. I steeled myself and stood firm. I watched the water. The last time I was here that was the moment I woke up and suspected that something was wrong with the lake.

What was meant to turn me away was turned around for good. I didn't know it at the time, but it was the start of this epic mission. Wait! Something was different. It was the light. This scene was not ominous, portending a coming storm. It was soft and bright, inviting like the pageantry preceding a coronation. Where was it coming from?

I sat on the beach casting my gaze toward the heavens. I was completely captivated, unable to look away from the gentle, serene light emanating from the clouds.

After some time, I finally got up and looked for five smooth stones. Satisfied I had found the right ones, I pulled the sling out of my back pocket and swirled it over my head to loosen up. I tried a few practice throws.

Feeling a surge of adrenaline, I marched back five more steps from the original spot. My challenge to hit the island with a stone had been denied by a storm. I'll show you!

With the steely stare of a pitcher staring down a batter, I pulled a stone out of my pocket and tossed it in the air several times, while slowly nodding my head, all the while staring down that oversized rock in the lake.

Finally ready, I loaded the stone in my sling. Like helicopter rotors churning into motion, I began to wind up, faster and faster. Feeling a final burst of adrenaline, I was set to release. But as I pulled the trigger, my front leg jolted sharply to the left, drastically changing the direction of the trajectory. The stone splashed harmlessly into the lake far off its mark.

What do you think you are doing? What are you trying to prove? I thought. *You are not that young, timid, troubled boy anymore.*

That young boy, armed only with what is in my hand right now, took down a goliath armed with a heavy sword. That same young man disarmed a principal and the king that was covering up his misdeeds.

Though they took away your honor and denied you your treasure, they failed! You took that imaginary ancient knight's sword that the principal mocked you with and turned it into a lightsaber. You thrust that saber into the lake where your rock just landed.

As the light spread from the saber, illuminating a wound, you angrily cried, "There, do you see it now?!" Five thousand people saw, and they won't forget.

Unknown to you, many others were watching. The Chippewa/Ojibwe and their ancestors, the aanikoobijigan, all took notice. Their spirits were revived when Mishipizheu broke into a smile as he slowly lowered his head. In that bow, a warrior was acknowledged, and a people were heard.

They didn't see the illuminated lake; they saw your sacrifice and your valor as you fought to protect their ancient traditions. They were pleased when they finally saw a white man follow the great Creator's protocol and take a stand to care for His creation and their lands.

Slowly dropping the sling, I realized I wasn't denied. I'd been recast. I'd become…

Suddenly, a slit appeared in the clouds, backlit with a soft, glowing light. The warmth signaled Ahne's unmistakable presence. With a growing smile, my eyes gazed into the heavens. As if in slow motion, a bright, narrow beam of light appeared through the slit. I followed the light as it descended to the lake. Playing tricks with my eyes, the light beam amazingly resembled an ancient sword.

When it hit the lake, the beam continued to spread, penetrating the surface and illuminating the lake as it grew. In breathless awe, I dropped to one knee and, as one drowning, stretched out my hand in the direction of the beam. When the connection occurred, all I could do was bow my head in grateful humility.

The boy had thrown stones. The man held a sword.

EPILOGUE

The real story of the "messy king" and Lake Superior is about Reserve Mining Company and the EPA, not the boy and Reserve. When they showed up as the posse a couple of years later, it was a national news story. This back story you read is akin to the story of the Dutch boy holding his finger in the dike until help arrived.

In 1969, the means to intervene and stop environmental damage of this kind were nonexistent. None of the states bordering Lake Superior, Minnesota, Wisconsin, or Michigan, had regulatory boards that could intervene. The County Health Departments, Lake County where Reserve was located, had some regulatory authority in the event of a public health threat, such as in the case of contaminated drinking water. (Ironically a serious health problem in the drinking water was discovered later when the EPA found asbestos in the lake water. That became a lead story on the national news! So, Dan and concerned classmates who drank right out of the lake, no, it's not safe to drink it like that.)

It would take an act of Congress to rescue the lake.

On January 1, 1970, the National Environmental Policy Act (NEPA) was signed into law by President Nixon. The EPA, armed with the Clean Air and Water Acts, was formed later in the fall. Almost immediately, the EPA started an investigation into the impact of Reserve's operation on the lake. It was the kind of investigation George wanted when he left the "speeding ticket" on Mr. Lee's desk.

To break down what followed, Reserve was one the EPA's first significant actions, and it resulted in the longest and costliest environmental trial in history. The trial started in 1973 and concluded in 1980. The plant was ordered to cease discharging its waste into Lake Superior.

After over forty-five years, the lake has healed itself. Today, a beautiful marina is situated near where the plant's river carried tons of sediment into the lake.

That part of the story has a happy conclusion. Unfortunately, the entire decade of the 1970s was a difficult time for thousands of families in Silver Bay, as the plant was mired in lawsuits and setbacks until it finally closed in 1986. All the jobs were lost.

Of course, George's father escaped the "dragon's" wrath. His ark came to rest on a mountain in Colorado, where he landed a job at a large brewery from which he would retire a decade later.

George ended up attending the University of Colorado, just not on a full-ride scholarship.

It seemed that scholarships were as elusive as his dreams. What wasn't elusive was going to college in Colorado, skiing, and learning about cowboys. The latter, not so much!

WHAT IS A SUPERIOR GUARDIAN?

This is the part I didn't expect to write.

When I first started *The Superior Guardian*, I thought I was writing about my past. But as I near the end, I see that I've been writing about something else: about us—about anyone who's ever had to rise again when life hit hard.

When I step back now and look at this story through the eyes of a reader, I see a coming-of-age tale about a troubled young immigrant boy who grows up, stands against injustice, and helps protect the great Lake Superior. By the end, he's honored with an almost mythical title: The Superior Guardian.

If I were reading this about someone else, I'd probably feel inspired.

If I were reading it about the author himself, I might raise an eyebrow.

"Nice story," I might think. "You wrote yourself into sainthood. Must be nice to give yourself a title."

And that's exactly why this section exists.

The truth is, the knight on the cover—the one kneeling—isn't a conqueror basking in glory. He's humbled. He kneels in gratitude, not victory. The title of Superior Guardian isn't a trophy; it's a trust. It's not earned by triumph but by transformation. And if you've read this far, that trust now passes to you.

We live in a culture that tries to comfort pain with a single label: Victim. It's handed out freely, almost like a medal. It's meant to show compassion, but it quietly robs something sacred—our dignity, our agency, our strength. Victimhood is the world's counterfeit for being seen. It says, "You poor thing," when what the soul really longs to hear is, "I see you. You're still standing."

A Superior Guardian is the antidote, the anthesis of victimhood.

A Superior Guardian is someone who refuses to be defined by pain or circumstance. Someone who stands watch over what is good and sacred, even when the world looks away. It isn't about being flawless or fearless—it's about remaining faithful in the storm.

My father was one. He left his homeland and brought his young family to a faraway country where he didn't speak the language, only to be told he couldn't have the job that brought him there. But instead of breaking, he adapted. He learned. He rose. He didn't wait for pity.

He forged a way forward. He wasn't a victim. He was a Guardian.

And maybe, so are you.

Because if you've endured—if you've faced loss, betrayal, heartbreak, or hardship—and you're still here, still reaching for light, still hoping and trying… then this title belongs to you, too.

You are not invisible.

You are not forgotten.

You are not what happened to you.

You are felt.

You are seen.

You are more than what was done to you.

You are a Superior Guardian.

And if you choose to claim that title, then the words on the next page are yours.

ARE YOU A SUPERIOR GUARDIAN?

A Superior Guardian is not defined by rank, wealth, or title. A Guardian is marked by courage forged in trial, truth spoken in the face of lies, and hope carried through nights that felt endless.

A Superior Guardian stands watch over what is sacred. They guard their families, their communities, and their world with quiet resolve. They are not perfect. They stumble. They fall. But they rise again scarred yet stronger, wounded yet wiser.

To be a Guardian is to live with integrity, to endure with faith, and to hold fast to what is good even when others let go. This identity is not given lightly. It is earned through perseverance, valor, and the refusal to quit when everything within whispers, "give up."

A Superior Guardian is anyone who has faced the waves of the storm, been knocked down by its fury, and chosen—again and again—to rise.

AUTHOR INVITATION – A GUARDIAN'S COMMISSION

If you have carried the crushing weight of life…
If you have endured the long night of the soul…
If you have risen again after being struck down—

You are not alone.

Your scars are not shame.
They are proof of your valor.
They are the mark of one who endures.

I extend to you a new name.
Not a trinket. Not a trophy.
But a mantle earned in fire:
Superior Guardian.

The Guardian's Creed
I stand with courage.
I guard with truth.
I endure with hope.

I am a Guardian.
I protect what is sacred.
I rise when others fall.

I stand firm in faith.

I guard my brothers and sisters.

I endure, for the battle belongs to the Lord.

This is your commission:

Stand for truth.

Guard what is sacred.

Rise again, even when the battle is not finished.

Carry this identity forward—

Into your family, your community, your world.

And when the shadows press in, remember:

You are not alone.

Welcome, fellow Guardian.

A PLACE TO BELONG

If these words have spoken to your heart, you are not alone. You now belong to a fellowship of Guardians who carry this same calling. We invite you to continue the journey with us in The Superior Guardian warrior community.

ABOUT THE AUTHOR

GEORGE GRIESINGER is a writer and musician whose life has been shaped by storms—both literal and personal. Born in Europe and raised in the United States, he grew up learning what it means to leave behind the familiar and walk into the unknown. That immigrant journey shaped his sense of faith, identity, and resilience—themes that run through *The Superior Guardian.*

Music has been a lifelong companion. In his early thirties, George led a worship band for young adults, and today he finds joy leading a guitar and singing group for active older adults at his local YMCA. At home, he continues to explore music privately with his helpmate, Susan, whose encouragement and creative vision helped bring The Superior Guardian to life.

Now widowed and retired, George devotes his days to writing, music, fitness, and faith. His debut book is both a personal story and an open invitation—to rise, to endure, and to discover the Guardian within.

To visit the author online, go to TheSuperiorGuardian.com.